ROLL

ROLL

DARCY MILLER

HARPER

An Imprint of HarperCollinsPublishers

ISBN 978-0-06-246122-3 (trade bdg.)

Typography by Katie Klimowicz

17 18 19 20 21   CG/LSCH   10 9 8 7 6 5 4 3 2 1

❖

First Edition

For my dad

CHAPTER 1

OKAY.

There are birds falling out of the sky.

I'm not an expert on bird behavior or anything, but I'm pretty sure birds aren't just supposed to *fall out of the sky*.

I mean, right? We can all agree that's weird?

Speaking of weird, my name is Lauren . . . and I'm a boy.

Pretty good segue, huh? Dad says I have a gift for changing the conversation. He's also the one who decided to call me Lauren, so I take his compliments with a grain of salt.

To be fair, I was named after my grandpa, who died

the week before I was born. Grandpa was six feet tall and a retired Navy SEAL, which means he was the kind of guy who could pull off a name like "Lauren."

I, on the other hand, am not.

For starters, I'm short. In fact, I'm the shortest eleven-year-old I know. I wear glasses. And read comics. Add that all up with the fact that one time, in gym class, David Stadler accidentally knocked me unconscious with a volleyball, and, well . . .

Just trust me; being named Lauren is the worst. Even though everyone calls me "Ren."

I've thought about it a lot over the years, and I'm pretty sure Grandpa would have agreed with me. If he could have talked at the end, he probably would have sat up on his deathbed and proclaimed something along the lines of, "Do not name your child 'Lauren,' my son. It's a terrible idea."

But I'm getting off topic here. The point is: *Birds are falling from the sky.*

Wait.

Birds *were* falling from the sky. I swear they were, just a second ago.

But now they're just kind of . . . there. Drifting above the neighbors' tree line and flying back and forth in a circle and acting like, well, *birds*.

Huh.

Maybe I'm imagining things.

Maybe all these years of being forced to answer to the name Lauren have finally driven me over the edge.

Maybe waking up at six a.m. on my summer vacation has cooked my brain.

Or maybe—oh, no, wait! They're doing it again!

I sit up from my spot in the grass, unsticking my sweaty "Free Bananaman" T-shirt from my back.

Bananaman is my favorite comic of all time. It was popular back in the eighties, in England, but shockingly no one's ever heard of it here in the US.

It's kind of ridiculous, but pretty funny, too. There's this kid named Eric Wimp, who's about my age, and when he eats a banana, he turns into this superhero named Bananaman. Bananaman has the strength of twenty men (twenty *big* men), and he fights all these supervillains who are kind of like joke versions of real supervillains, like Doctor Gloom and Skunk Woman. He has a fortress in the North Pole that's shaped like a giant banana.

Like I said, it's ridiculous.

I push my glasses up the bridge of my nose for a better look at the birds. I can't wear contacts, because the idea of touching my eyeball makes me feel gross.

It turns out I was wrong; the birds aren't really falling out of the sky. They're more . . . *somersaulting*.

Like someone is sending a secret message to them, telling them to stop flying, freeze in midair for a second, and then throw themselves backward toward the ground like weird, feathery little gymnasts.

I tense up a little as the kamikaze birds near the tree line. But just as I think they're about to hit the ground, the little dudes swoop upward again, like nothing ever happened.

It's definitely weird.

But what's *really* weird is that it happens again.

And again.

And again.

I'm just starting to worry there's something seriously wrong with the birds (some new, highly infectious, and awesome strain of avian flu, maybe) when the screen door scrapes open against the porch with a loud *screeeeek*.

Dad's been saying he's going to fix the door ever since we moved out to the country.

It's strange, living in Grandma's old house. Like it's not really ours. The bathrooms still smell like her potpourri, her umbrella still sits in its stand next to the door, and Grandpa's Distinguished Service Medal still hangs on the wall.

At our old house, in town, the door didn't stick. The bathrooms smelled like Lysol, and we never used umbrellas.

Westville is only eight miles away but sometimes it feels like a million.

I turn to look at the door and see Dad. He owns his own structural engineering firm, so usually he just wears a button-down shirt to work, but he's meeting some big new client in Fairmont later this morning. He looks strange in a suit.

"Hey, kiddo. How was your run?"

Exhausting. Boring. Painful.

"Great," I lie. "Look at these birds."

Dad leans against the door frame. "Did you concentrate on your foot strikes?"

Do you know how hard it is to concentrate on your foot strikes while you're running? It's like trying to pat your stomach and rub your head at the same time. Only sweatier. "Look," I say again, trying to distract him. "The birds are acting really weird."

Dad steps onto the porch, holding the screen door open with his size thirteen foot. Unlike me, everything about Dad is big. He raises his hand to shield his eyes against the sun. "What birds?"

"Over there." I point across the field, which slopes downward from our yard until it meets the neighbors' tree line. Their house is probably about a mile away, if you use the roads. Shorter if you cut through the field, kitty-corner.

There's nothing there.

I mean, the trees are there, obviously. Blue sky, a few clouds, the sun are all accounted for. It's not like a giant black hole suddenly opened up above the neighbors' house or anything.

But the birds are gone.

"They were right there," I say, staring at the patch of empty sky. Birds couldn't just vanish into thin air, could they?

"Must have flown away," Dad says, dragging me back to the real world. "Come on in. Mom and I have to leave soon."

I wince as he pulls the screen door shut again, seemingly oblivious to its screech.

Maybe Dad is right. Maybe the birds flew away. But that doesn't explain where they went. Or what they were doing before they disappeared.

I sit for another minute, waiting to see if they'll reappear.

"Ren?" Dad's voice drifts through the open door. "What's the holdup, kiddo?"

Reluctantly, I push myself to my feet. With a final backward glance at the sky, I head for the house.

CHAPTER 2

IF YOU EVER want to freak yourself out, try Googling "birds falling from the sky" sometime.

It's pretty disturbing stuff.

At least worrying about accidental pesticide poisoning (one reason birds might randomly fall from the sky) gives me something new to focus on during my morning run the next day. Usually, I just count telephone poles and try not to think about the gnats flying up my nose.

By the time I turn around to start back home, though, even the threat of off-target contaminate drifting can't keep the boredom at bay. After all, this is Southern Minnesota. If you find soybean fields fascinating, you're in luck. If not, well . . . Let's just say I haven't been feeling particularly lucky lately.

I know that this whole "joining the cross-country team" thing was my idea to begin with, but I guess I thought running was going to be a little more . . . fun. Honestly, I have no idea why Dad likes it so much.

My breath comes in short, sharp pants as I struggle up the hill. I can feel a side ache coming on. Hunching over, I ball my fist and press it against my stomach, trying to ease the cramp.

I probably look like Quasimodo with diarrhea. For once, I'm glad we moved to the middle of nowhere.

I finally make it past the hill to the intersection and turn back onto our road. I'm almost home when a flicker of movement catches my eye. Peering across the field, I see a dozen or so birds swoop into sight. They're flying right over the neighbors' house again.

I stagger to a stop.

Sucking air (and the occasional gnat) through my nose, I stare up at them, waiting to see if they're going to start somersaulting again.

A long minute passes.

My side hurts. Sweat drips down my neck. Mosquitoes descend on me like some sort of all-you-can-eat buffet.

The birds keep circling.

I'm just about to give up when it happens; pitching suddenly backward, the birds tumble downward, plummeting into the trees.

I'm not about to let them disappear again.

Without stopping to think, I plunge into the long grass at the side of the road. Half running, half stumbling, I make my way down into the ditch and up to the other side. My feet sink into the ground as I cut across the field to the neighbors' property.

By the time I reach the tree line, I'm out of breath again, and my running shoes are covered with some serious mud.

Up close, the trees aren't as thick as they look from the road. I can see flashes of blue sky through the branches. The ground is covered in fallen pine needles.

It smells kind of like Christmas dinner. With a side of fertilizer.

Peering through the trees, I check out the neighbors' house. We haven't met them yet. What if they're the kind of people with dogs? Or with guns? Or both?

The white, shingled farmhouse looks a lot like ours, only the neighbors' paint is peeling in places, and the grass of their lawn is just a tiny bit too long. There's a red station wagon parked in the driveway with a bunch of faded bumper stickers on the back.

I squint, trying to make out the writing. You can tell

a lot about a person from their choice of bumper stickers. Luckily, the ones on the neighbors' car seem okay. There's one that says "Wage Peace," which I take as a good sign I won't be shot on sight for trespassing.

Fingers crossed, anyway.

In the field behind the house, a section of weeds has been mown down into stubble. There's a small building in the middle, about the size of Grandma's old gardening shed. In fact, it *looks* just like Grandma's gardening shed, except for the wire cage sitting on top of the roof.

There are birds in it, I realize, peering closer. Just a couple of them, from what I can see.

A girl about my age steps out of the shed's door, and I dodge behind the nearest tree trunk. I can hear my blood pounding in my ears. Adrenaline whips through my veins.

This is probably what superheroes feel like all the time.

I force myself to count to twenty. Then I shift my weight, peeking around the edge of the tree trunk.

Superheroes probably don't peek. I'll bet the word "peek" isn't even in their vocabulary.

To be fair, they aren't real, so their vocabulary is probably pretty limited.

"What are you doing?"

I freeze, my arms curled around the tree trunk like I'm in love with it, or something.

Dendrophilia, a tiny part of my brain whispers. *Romantic interest in trees.*

The girl from the shed is standing just a few feet away, staring at me.

Her hair is red. Really, really red. Unnaturally red. There are some stripes of bright yellow in there, too, and orange.

Being reasonably smart for my age, I deduce that she's dyed it.

I've never met anyone our age with dyed hair before.

It looks cool. Like lava, flowing over the shoulders of her black T-shirt. Like her hair is erupting out of her head.

We're still staring at each other. She's skinny, almost as skinny as me, with a pointy chin and dark blue eyes. Her denim cutoffs are covered with black scribbles. A Sharpie marker from the looks of it. The words are all upside down. Like she got bored, and wrote on her shorts while she was wearing them.

Mom would kill me if I wrote on my shorts with a Sharpie.

The girl's gaze flicks past my shoulder. I turn to look, too. As the birds tumble down in another round of backflips, she raises her hand, holding a thing that looks like a tape measure, only smaller. She clicks it again and again.

She's wearing black nail polish, I notice. It's chipped. I suddenly feel out of my league.

"Are you lost?" The girl's voice is surprisingly scratchy. It sounds like the way Velcro feels, if that makes sense.

I push myself away from the tree, wiping my palms on the front of my running shorts. "Um . . . I was running."

She looks at me, obviously waiting for me to say more.

"I saw the birds, and . . ." I trail off, trying to think of what to say next.

"Do you live around here?" the girl asks, still clicking.

"We just moved." I point toward the hill, at Grandma's house. Or our house, I guess. "From town. I'm not new, or anything."

"I am," the girl says bluntly. She reaches down to scratch a mosquito bite on her leg. "We moved last month. From DC. My name's Sutton, by the way. Sutton Davies."

Sutton. Sutton Davies.

"Lauren," I say, bracing myself for the inevitable response. "Lauren Hall." I wait for the laughter to start.

Sutton just looks at me. "Lauren?"

I nod.

"Have you ever thought about going by your middle name?"

As if that solution had never occurred to me before. "I don't have one."

She shrugs. "You're not missing much. Mine's Priscilla."

Priscilla. Sutton Priscilla Davies.

I don't know. It has a certain ring to it.

"Most people call me Ren," I explain.

Above us, the birds launch backward again. Sutton raises her hand, clicking the little gadget. "Why do they do that?" I ask.

Sutton keeps her eyes on the birds. "They're Birmingham Roller pigeons. That's what they do."

Wait. "Pigeons? You have pigeons as *pets*?"

"They're not pets." Sutton drops her gaze back to me, lifting her chin. "I'm training them. They're going to be *champions*."

CHAPTER 3

UM . . . okay.

Is it even possible to train pigeons? Aren't pigeons basically vermin? It'd be like training squirrels. Only harder, because pigeons could fly away from you. Although there are flying squirrels, I guess. But I don't think they actually fly. Or do they?

"Training them to do what?" I ask.

My voice sounds weird. I'm using the same tone Mom used with Grandma near the end, after Grandma moved to the Sunny Pines "retirement community" and sometimes thought the nurses were stealing her socks.

Sutton raises her arm again, clicking rapidly on the thingy in her hand as the birds fall through the air.

"That," she says, motioning upward.

"You're teaching them to somersault?"

"It's called 'rolling.' And they already know how to do it." Sutton pushes her hair back from her face. Even in the shade, the colors seem to glow. Like her head isn't just any volcano. It's a radioactive one.

"But if they already know what they're doing, then why are you training them?" I ask.

"I'm trying to get the kit to break together. You want them to roll as long as possible, and . . ." She trails off. "It's kind of complicated."

"Oh. Okay." I can't help wondering what she was going to say next.

The birds seem to be slowing down now. A few of them are occasionally still "rolling," but they're mostly just flying back and forth above the trees.

"So what grade are you in?" Sutton asks.

Technically, since there are four weeks left of summer vacation, I'm not in *any* grade. But Mom says pointing out that sort of information is, quote, "being obnoxious for the sake of being obnoxious" and "will probably not earn you any friends."

Mom has a lot of wisdom like that.

"I'm going into sixth," I say aloud. "I'm eleven."

Sutton nods. "Me, too. Do you know who your teacher is?"

"Mr. Weinholt."

"I have Mrs. Thompson," Sutton says. "Do you know anything about her?"

"I think she's in PEO with my mom. I don't really know her, though. She seems okay. She smiles a lot."

Sutton tilts her head to one side. Her left, specifically. "What's PEO?"

"This club. I'm not really sure what they do."

"Well, what does PEO stand for?"

"I don't know," I say honestly. "It's a secret." Their Wikipedia page doesn't even say.

She looks vaguely impressed. "Your mom's in a secret club?"

"Not a *secret* secret club," I explain. "She's not, like, a Freemason, or anything." Do they even let women become Freemasons? I make a mental note to look it up later. That and flying squirrels. "They do potlucks and have educational speakers, and stuff," I tell Sutton. "I think they give out college scholarships, too."

She considers this for a second. "Oh. Sounds kind of boring."

I feel a flicker of something pass through me. Just because Mom's club *sounds* boring doesn't mean someone should *say* it sounds boring. Even I know that's rude.

To my surprise, I feel my mouth opening. "Well, I

don't think anyone's asking you to join."

Uh-oh.

I'm suddenly very aware of the fact that Sutton is at least two inches taller than me. Most people my age are at least two inches taller than me. Especially girls. And Sutton looks as though she could hold her own in a fight. Maybe it's the hair. It's kind of . . . fierce, you know?

Luckily, Sutton doesn't seem mad.

"Oh." Sutton looks up again, clicking her little counter thingy as some of the pigeons roll again. I wince as one of them gets a little too close to the ground.

"Do they ever, um . . ." I search for the right word. "Splat?"

She stares at me.

I take it that's a no.

"How long will they stay up there?" I ask, hoping to redeem myself. She looks down at her watch. It's big, with a wide, leather strap. It looks old.

I've never seen anyone our age wearing a watch before, either.

"They should be coming down soon," she says. "It depends. Sometimes, they—"

"Sutton, honey? Are you out there?" It's a woman's voice. Sutton's mom, I'm guessing.

Sutton pauses mid-sentence, turning to look back at her house.

"I should go," I say. I've almost forgotten about the fact I'm supposed to be running right now. Dad is probably wondering about my time.

"All right." Sutton shrugs. "See you around."

"See you around." With a final glance at the pigeons, I take off toward home.

CHAPTER 4

THE SCREEN DOOR screeches as usual, announcing my presence before I'm even inside.

"Morning, honey," Mom calls from the kitchen. She glances up from her phone as I walk in, gesturing at the box of frozen waffles on the counter behind her. "There's breakfast."

Mom looks tired.

I didn't hear her car pull up last night. She's Westville's only veterinarian, which means she's pretty much always on call. Even in the middle of the night. Or halfway through her son's first (and only) theater performance.

To be fair, I played a tree. And it was in the first grade.

Still, it's a useful fact to bring up once in a while.

"Hey, kiddo. Did you mark your miles?" Dad hurries into the kitchen, pouring himself a giant thermos of coffee. The thermos looks small in his hands. Seriously, his hands are so big he can palm a basketball.

My running log is taped to the freezer door. Grabbing a pen from the counter, I walk over to the piece of graph paper. Dad came up with the idea for the chart years ago, when he used to coach cross-country. Three miles equals a straight line. More than three miles, and the line slants upward. Less than three, it goes down.

Despite my best efforts, my line graph is currently seven boxes below its starting point.

As I draw a straight line through the next box, Dad says, "You know, if you want, I could go for some runs with you in the evenings. It might be a good way to get your totals up."

I nod, pretending to think about it. "Yeah, maybe."

I can tell Dad is disappointed in my graph.

I'm disappointed, too.

I don't understand what happened. I mean, it's not like I didn't do my research. I subscribed to *Runner's World*. I watched dozens of instructional videos online. I learned how to keep my hands in unclenched fists, like I'm carrying potato chips without crushing them, and how to hold my arms at a ninety-degree angle. I spent *two days* researching the brand of shoe with the most accommodating toe box.

I prepared for everything.

Except for the part where I actually had to, you know . . . *run.*

To be honest, I'm actually starting to think twice about joining the cross-country team this fall. Not that I'm planning on telling Dad about that; he'd be crushed. Ever since I mentioned I was thinking of trying out for the team, he's been going around using phrases like "the apple doesn't fall far from the tree" and calling me a "chip off the old block."

I think he's just excited we finally have something to talk about over dinner.

I lower the pen. "Can you take me to Three Men this afternoon? There's a new issue of *Inferior Five* in for me. Well, an old one. From 1968." *Inferior Five* is another one of my favorite comics, about these five superheroes who have these pretty much useless powers. Like, the Blimp can fly, but only really, really slowly, and Awkwardman can live underwater, but when he's on land, he has to keep watering himself with a gardening can.

Anyway, Three Men and a Comic Book is this awesome comic book store in Rochester, which is about twenty minutes away. My best friend, Aiden, and I go there all the time. Mike, the owner, knows us by name and everything.

"Which one is *Inferior Five* again?" Dad asks. "The one with Bunny Girl?"

"Dumb Bunny," I correct him. Also known as Athena Tremor, daughter of Princess Power.

Dad slaps his thigh. "Dumb Bunny. That's right. 'Strong as an ox, and almost as smart,'" he says triumphantly.

"Right," I say, humoring him.

He waggles his eyebrows challengingly. "Quick, what's the name of her sister?"

"Half sister," I say. "And it's Angel. Angel Beatrix O'Day. So can you take me to Three Men?"

Dad gives an exaggerated sigh of defeat because I won his latest round of comic trivia, then shakes his head. "No can do, kiddo. I'm on site in Fairmont all day. That strip mall I was telling you about. Sorry."

"Sorry for what?" Mom asks, still scrolling through the messages on her phone.

"Ren wants to go to the cartoon store later."

"Comics."

"What?"

I toss the pen back on the countertop. I can already see where this is going. "It's a comic book store. Not cartoons." Which he would know, if he actually read them instead of just looking up stuff on the internet.

Not that there's anything wrong with looking stuff up on the internet. As far as I'm concerned, the internet is mankind's single greatest achievement.

See also: fire, the wheel, and microwave pizza rolls.

Dad rolls his eyes jokingly in Mom's direction. "Comics," he mouths.

Mom purses her lips. "Sorry, honey. Back-to-back surgeries at eleven thirty. Could we go now?"

"They don't open until nine."

"I could take you tomorrow," Dad chimes in. "Any time. Besides, if you've waited fifty years to read this one, what's another day?"

I get that Dad's busy, but sometimes it feels like I'm always waiting for another day. Like this spring, when he promised to take me to see the *Journey through Space* exhibit at the science museum. By the time he had a free day, it was closed. Ditto the Renaissance Faire, last summer.

I was really looking forward to those giant turkey legs, too.

"Okay. Thanks," I tell Dad. Opening the fridge, I grab a soda.

"Hey, what do you think you're doing?" Mom asks, raising her eyebrows. "No soda before three o'clock, you know that."

I set the Dr Pepper back down on the refrigerator shelf with more force than is strictly necessary.

Behind my back, I can feel Mom and Dad exchanging a glance. They're doing that silent telecommunication thing where they decide which one of them is going to speak first.

It's Dad. "Sorry we've been gone so much lately, kiddo. Things'll slow down once the summer's over."

"Hey, tomorrow's Tuesday," Mom adds. "Aiden's still coming over to help with the basement, right?"

If we lived in town, I wouldn't need to *plan* hanging out with my best friend. Aiden's house was a five-minute walk from ours. I could see him every day if I wanted to. In fact, I pretty much *did* see him every day.

"Shoot, is that the time?" Mom pushes back her chair. "I have an endoscopy in fifteen minutes!"

"I should head out, too," Dad says. Tightening the lid on his thermos, he holds the door open for Mom, who's busy shoving things into her bag.

"Have a good day," Mom calls. "Don't rot your brain too much!"

I wait until I can hear the crunch of their cars disappearing up the gravel driveway. Grabbing the Dr Pepper from the fridge, I glance out the window.

The sky above Sutton's house is empty.

CHAPTER 5

"YO."

I stare up at the slanted ceiling, trying to not yawn. Aiden's call woke me up from a nap, and the edge of my pillow is wet. For some reason, I only drool when I sleep during the day, never at night.

"Did you know people have been saying 'yo' since the fifteenth century?" I ask Aiden. "Seriously. Back in the day, people were probably like, 'Yo, Shakespeare! What doth be up?'"

It's hot in my room. Mom and Dad *claim* they're putting in central air, but right now, the box fan in my window is my only defense against heatstroke. I hold the phone a little away from my ear, flapping the neck of my T-shirt open and closed.

I sneak a quick peek down the front, just in case.

No chest hair yet.

"You're still coming over tomorrow, aren't you?" I ask. My parents are paying Aiden and me five dollars an hour each to go through all my grandparents' boxes in the basement. So far the most exciting thing we've found has been a dead mouse.

Frankly, I think we need a raise.

"Yeah," Aiden says. "Hey, you haven't talked to Kurt, have you?"

Kurt.

Have I talked to Kurt?

Have I *ever* talked to Kurt?

"Kurt Richardson?" I ask, just to make sure.

"Do you know anyone else named Kurt?" Aiden sounds impatient.

"Umm . . ." I say, thinking hard. "Give me a minute."

"Yes, Kurt Richardson," Aiden says.

I shake my head, even though Aiden can't see me. "Why would I talk to Kurt Richardson?"

Kurt Richardson is cool. Which sounds like a weird thing to say, but it's true. He does jackknives off the high board. He plays basketball. He drinks European soda that his mom has to order on Amazon for him. I do none of those things.

"He's having this huge party the last weekend in August," Aiden says, like it's the most natural thing in the world for him to be talking about Kurt Richardson's extracurricular activities. "Like a back-to-school sort of thing. His parents put in an aboveground pool."

I bring the phone in a little tighter, pressing it against my ear. "Have you guys been hanging out, or something?"

On the other end of the line, I can picture Aiden shrugging. He's probably sitting in his dad's armchair, swiveling back and forth as he talks.

"Some. At the pool."

Aiden and Kurt Richardson have been hanging out. At the pool. A strange feeling spreads through my body. I push myself up, swinging my legs over the side of the bed. "The normal pool? Or his aboveground pool?" I demand.

"What? Why? Does it matter?"

Yes. No. Maybe.

"Never mind," I say aloud. "Um, no. I haven't talked to Kurt. How would he even have our number?"

"You should get a cell phone, dude. It's weird, not being able to text you."

As if the thought of getting a cell phone had never occurred to me before. Mom and Dad have some sort of ridiculous theory that I shouldn't be allowed to have one until I'm fourteen.

"So Kurt's having a party? And I'm invited?"

There's a nanosecond of silence before Aiden replies. "Yeah. He said it was totally cool to bring people."

I let this sink in for a second.

"Totally cool to bring people? So he didn't actually invite me? I'm, like, your plus one, or something?"

"It's not a wedding. Okay? Relax."

Relax.

Aiden never used to tell me to relax.

I nod, even though he can't see me. "Okay. Sounds . . . fun."

It does *not* sound fun. I hope I don't actually have to go into the pool. I still plug my nose when I go underwater.

"I should go," Aiden tells me. "I've got to pee."

"And I've got to Q," I say automatically. It's a joke we made up when we were little. Because Q comes after P in the alphabet.

I never said it was a good joke.

I wait for the laughter from the other end of the line. Aiden's laugh is surprisingly deep, for someone who's barely twelve. It used to sound really funny, back when he was short like me and carrying around about twenty extra pounds. *Roly-poly*, Mom used to call him.

That was before he had his growth spurt last spring. He grew four inches in three months. According to Mom, he's *solid* now.

Like a rock.

Or a Chevy.

Or someone who hangs out with Kurt Richardson.

Aiden's silence seems very loud in my bedroom.

"*Q?*" I say again. "R, S, T, U, V?"

"Right." Aiden sounds distracted. "*Q.*"

I stare down at the hardwood floor, picking out the individual scars in the boards. For some reason, my throat feels weird, like there's something stuck back there. Probably a Cheeto. I was snacking on them earlier.

"Okay. Catch you later, man."

I swallow, but the lump is still there. "Catch you later."

So Aiden's hanging out with Kurt, I tell myself. So what? I've been missing in action all summer; Aiden's needed *someone* to hang out with. But school starts next month. Everything will go back to normal then.

It's probably not even worth thinking about.

As I toss the landline onto my nightstand, I glance out the window. The roof of Sutton's house is just visible.

I grab my laptop. What did she call her pigeons? Something-ham rollers?

I Google *roll pigeons*. The first page listed is a Wikipedia entry for "Birmingham Rollers."

Bingo.

I click on the link.

A picture of a pigeon pops up in the upper left-hand corner of the screen. A stumpy guy with short legs and tiny, perfectly round eyes. His back and wings are mostly gray, and his tail feathers are white with black stripes. But it's his neck that I find myself staring at. Flecks of purple, teal, and silver reflect in the light, cascading down from the crown of his head to the top of his back.

It's pretty cool-looking, actually.

Tearing my eyes away from the picture, I start to read. Birmingham Rollers originally came from Birmingham, England. Over the years, people trained them to somersault backward by breeding the ones who rolled together with one another. There's something called Parlor Rollers, too, only they spin backward on the ground.

I pull up a video of a bird spinning down a grassy lawn, thunking lopsidedly as it rolls. It looks like a drunk, feathery bowling ball.

It's awesome.

No one is quite sure why the birds roll to begin with, I learn, going back to Wikipedia. Some people think they do it to evade predators. Other people think it's a genetic defect. A few people think they do it just for fun.

I like the last theory.

I'm just clicking on a video of a pigeon rolling in slow

motion when I hear the crunch of Mom's car on the driveway. My stomach growls in response.

I can't help it. All I had for lunch was Cheetos.

I go to shut my laptop, suddenly realizing I didn't tell Aiden about Sutton or her birds.

Weird.

CHAPTER 6

"KIDDO?" DAD'S KNOCK practically rattles the door off its frame. "It's six o'clock!"

I pull my pillow over my ears, groaning.

"Are you up? Are your feet touching the floor?"

"Yes!" I shout.

There's a pause.

"Liar!" Dad calls cheerfully. And then the knocking starts again. It grows louder and louder until, finally, I can't stand it anymore.

It's a dirty trick. The police use the same technique sometimes, during hostage situations.

Throwing the pillow against the wall, I push myself out of bed and fling open the door. It's less dramatic than it sounds, since the door thunks against an unpacked moving box and just kind of stops halfway.

"Satisfied?" I ask.

Dad grins at me from the doorway, his coffee thermos in hand. "You're the one who wanted me to wake you up so you could train," he points out.

I try to rub some of the sleep out of my eyes. "You know, the peak time for running isn't actually first thing in the morning. Your body temperature is low, your lung function is poor, your energy stores are depleted . . ."

Dad ignores me. "That's the spirit!" Giving my bicep an encouraging thump, he wanders down the hallway.

I stare after him, rubbing my arm.

Ten minutes later, I'm standing in the front yard, trying to stretch my quads as Dad's Subaru crunches down the driveway.

As Dad turns the corner, I reluctantly start jogging. The early-morning sun is already hot on my shoulders, and the tag of my T-shirt feels scratchy against my neck.

I stumble over a loose rock, nearly biting it on the side of the road. "Heel, toe," I tell myself, trying to concentrate on the way my foot lands on the ground. *Thinking* about running while you're *actually* running is tricky.

As I head down the hill, nearing Sutton's driveway, my pace slows.

Just a little.

Then a little more.

And a little more.

Finally, I stop altogether. Dropping to one knee, I bend to check my shoelace. Running with a loose shoelace can lead to injury.

I'm pretty sure.

As I carefully re-loop my bow, I make a deal with myself. I'm going to look up, just once. If Sutton's pigeons are out, it'll be a sign. And if not, well . . . That'll be a sign, too, I guess.

I raise my head.

Except for a few clouds, the sky is empty.

I can't help feeling a twinge of disappointment. But just as I'm about to take my first step, I hear a screen door slamming in the distance. Something bright red flashes through the trees.

Sutton's hair.

Feeling like a trespasser (which, technically, I am), I lope up her driveway. As I hit the edge of the tree line, I veer off, heading for the field. I make it to the edge of the clearing just in time to see Sutton fiddling with a little door on the side of the shed. She swings it open, revealing a hole in the side of the shed about six inches wide. The hole is lined with thin, metal bars, almost like a tiny jail cell.

Sutton steps back.

Pigeons surge forward, pressing their heads against the bottom of the metal bars, which swing outward in response. The birds flap upward out of the hole in a confusion of gray and white wings. Sutton tilts her head back. She's wearing a battered Nationals baseball cap. It's too big, but I can see why she wears it. It's *bright* out here. I bring my hand up, squinting against the early-morning glare.

I'll just watch for a minute, and then I'll get back to my run.

The birds swoop upward, circling one another in widening arcs. I stand hidden in the trees like some sort of hermit. *Anthropophobia*, I think. *The fear of people.*

The birds are gathering closer to one another now, flying back and forth in a pack. Still, none of them are . . . rolling . . . yet. Maybe they don't do it every time they fly. Maybe they're just going to do laps today.

But a second later, one of the pigeons tumbles backward, dropping through the sky. The others follow suit.

Well, most of them, anyway.

Not all of them actually roll at the same time. A few stragglers just kind of float around, waiting for the rest to catch up with them. Like maybe they think the others won't notice.

It's a pretty good strategy. I've used it in gym class.

I stare up at the birds, my eyes watering in the sunlight. Even though I know it's coming, I still feel a little blip of excitement every time they roll. I wonder if this is what people who watch sports feel like every time someone scores a point.

"I thought I was the only not sleeping in on summer vacation."

At the sound of Sutton's voice, I guiltily drop my gaze from the birds. She waves pointedly at me.

Great. So much for being hidden.

I make my way toward the shed, my feet dragging a little. "Sorry," I say, feeling stupid. "I didn't mean to spy."

"Let me guess," Sutton says, pointing toward my legs. "You were out running again?"

I look down at my athletic shorts. They're black, and knee-length, and kind of shiny. They make a strange whisking noise every time I move.

"Um, yeah. I'm going out for cross-country in the fall."

As the birds launch into another roll, Sutton looks up over my shoulder, clicking away at her little tape measure thing. "You like to run?" she asks distractedly.

I nudge the toe of my running shoe against a clod of dirt. "Yeah. I guess. I mean, I'm not really sure yet. It's only been eight weeks."

Sutton looks dubious. "You've been doing it for eight weeks and you're still not sure if you like it?"

"I *will* like it," I insist. "I just need to build up my endurance a little more." And somehow figure out a way to make the actual running part less . . . terrible. Maybe I should start listening to audiobooks. I make a mental note to check out the library's collection. "My dad was a cross-country coach for a long time," I tell Sutton. "He says the secret to running is running."

Sutton's grin is surprising, but in a good way. "My dad says the secret to rolling pigeons is luck. Hey, do you want an Oreo?" she asks suddenly. "I keep a bag in the coop."

I hesitate. I should say no. Get back to my run before my quad muscles stiffen and fall off, or whatever.

"Sure," I hear myself saying. "Thanks."

"No prob." Sutton points toward a dilapidated lawn chair. As she disappears into the shed, I lower myself into the blue-and-white-striped chair.

After all, I can always run later.

CHAPTER 7

SUTTON HOLDS THE package up. "Want any more?"

I've already had eight. "Maybe just one," I say, reaching for the bag. When you think about it, there are worse things in the world than too many cookies. Unless you're diabetic, I guess.

I love Oreos. Usually, I unscrew the top and lick the frosting out first, then kind of weld the two halves back together with spit before I eat them.

Something tells me Sutton would be grossed out by this, though. Mom would call this "situational awareness." Dad would just say "common sense." Either way, I think I've made the right decision.

"So what's your story?" Sutton asks. She takes off

her baseball cap, scratching the top of her head. Her strange-colored hair ripples over her shoulders.

Ripples over her shoulders. I'm a real poet today.

I pull my eyes away. "I don't know," I admit. "I don't really have a story."

"You know, like, what do your parents do? How long have you lived here? Do you have any brothers or sisters?" Sutton asks, rattling the questions off rapid-fire.

"Um, my mom's a vet, and my dad works in construction. We used to live in town, but we just moved into my grandma's old house. And no, I'm an only child."

"Me, too," Sutton says. "It's great, right?"

"Being an only child?"

"Yeah. I mean, can you imagine having to share your room with someone? Although maybe if I had brothers and sisters my parents would be more relaxed. Like, whenever I screw up, they act like it's some huge tragedy, or a cry for help, or something. Like *everyone* hasn't gotten detention before."

I shift uncomfortably in my chair. Partially because the chair is uncomfortable, but mainly because *I've* never had detention. I've never even been close.

Sutton catches my expression. "It wasn't a big deal," she says hurriedly. "This kid at my old school was being a jerk. Grabbing my phone, and stuff. I was just taking it back, and he fell. He told everyone I shoved him."

I push my glasses up the bridge of my nose. "But you didn't?"

She grins. Two huge dimples appear on either side of her cheeks. They're very symmetrical.

"Maybe just a little," she confesses. "But he totally deserved it. Anyway, that's when my dad got the idea for the pigeons. I think he read some article about the importance of parent–child bonding, or something."

I glance around the clearing. One chair, one water bottle . . . For something that's supposed to be a bonding activity, Sutton seems to spend a lot of time doing it by herself. "So does he work mornings then? Your dad?"

"No. He's in the hospital. Mayo."

I blink. The Mayo Clinic is in Rochester. It's kind of famous, as far as hospitals go.

"Is he . . ." I trail off. I don't really know what I'm asking.

"He was in a car accident. Right after we got here. His legs are pretty screwed up," Sutton says matter-of-factly. Her voice sounds totally normal. Like we're chitchatting about the weather.

The Oreos feel heavy in my stomach all of a sudden.

"So he's going to be okay? How long does he have to stay in the hospital?"

Sutton shrugs. "They don't know. At least another

couple of weeks, while he starts rehab, and then we'll go from there. He'll be in a wheelchair, so we'll need to put in ramps, and stuff, too," she says, looking up toward the house. "My mom's pretty stressed."

I search through the corners of my brain, looking for the right thing to say.

Whatever it is, I can't seem to find it.

Sutton grins a little, obviously amused by the look on my face. "Look, do me a favor and don't get all weird about it, okay? He's going to be fine."

"Okay," I say, relieved.

"Cool," Sutton says. "Thanks."

It feels like a good time to change the subject. I stand up, Oreo crumbs raining to the ground. "Can I see inside the shed?"

"The coop?" Sutton shrugs. "Yeah, if you want. It's not that interesting."

The shed, or coop, as it's apparently called, looks like your standard eight-by-ten gardening shed. Mom would call it "a soothing shade of taupe." Dad would say it was brown.

I point toward the flat roof of the coop, where the separate, smaller wire cage is sitting. There are two pigeons inside. "Why are they in there?" I ask. "Did they do something wrong?"

Sutton grins again. "What, like pigeon jail? No, the

guy we buy our supplies from, in Rochester, is a fancier, too. He knows Dad and I are just getting started, so the last time we were there he gave me a couple of squeakers. It was really nice of him."

"Fancier? Squeaker?" I have no idea what Sutton is talking about. "Is there some sort of secret pigeon code I don't know about?" I ask.

She laughs.

"Fanciers are people who raise pigeons. It sounds ridiculous, I know. I think it's from, like, the eighteen-hundreds. And squeakers are just young birds," she clarifies. "I'm letting them settle in before I start flying them. They've been watching the rest of the kit fly, so they should know what to do." She looks worried. "At least I hope so."

She leads the way around the side of the coop, unlatching a small metal hook. Pulling open the plywood door, she pushes another, inner screen door to the side with her foot. "Home sweet home," she tells me, stepping inside.

I follow her into the shed, blinking a little at the dimness. Sutton reaches out, and the room fills with light. "Batteries," she explains, tapping the touch light mounted to the wall. "There's no electricity out here. Obviously."

The inside of the coop smells warm, and dusty, and

somehow . . . alive. The shed is divided into two small rooms, separated by a wire wall with a built-in door. The part we're standing in looks like a storeroom. Several clipboards full of paperwork are tacked up on the wall, and a shelf hangs to my right, its racks jumbled full of half-empty bottles, pens, and, for some reason, bingo daubers. I recognize the fat, colored marker thingies from when we used to visit Grandma at the retirement home.

She was strangely good at bingo. Almost too good. Like she'd somehow figured out a way to cheat, or something.

"We make our own feed," Sutton says, gesturing to the heavy-duty paper bags leaning up against the wall on my other side. "Field peas, wheat, safflower, and milo," she tells me, ticking off each bag with her finger. "You should see what they put in store-bought pigeon feed. It's like junk food."

I step closer to the wire partition. I assume the birds live on the other side, when they're not out flying. Small boxes for the pigeons to sleep in line the far wall. A false floor made of wire sits about an inch above the real floor, which is made of wood.

It's entirely covered in poop.

White poop, gray poop, brown poop . . . I've never seen so much poop before in my life.

I'm oddly impressed.

You'd think all that poop would make the coop smell, well . . . *terrible* . . . but for some reason, it doesn't. In fact, it's kind of a pleasant smell, in a way.

It's hard to explain.

"The floor pulls out," Sutton tells me. "It makes it easier to clean. Here, let me show you." Leading the way outside, she crouches down and tugs at a piece of plywood protruding from the bottom of the shed. It slides out easily, like a baking sheet from an oven.

Maybe that's not the best analogy.

"So you're training the pigeons by yourself?" I ask. "While your dad's . . . gone?"

"Yeah. He owes me big-time."

"So when's the World Cup?" I ask. "That's the big competition, right?"

Sutton looks up at me suspiciously. "How do you know about the World Cup?"

I don't blush, exactly. There is, however, the distinct possibility that my cheeks feel slightly warmer than usual. "I kind of looked some stuff up on the internet," I admit. Great. Now she probably thinks I'm some sort of weird internet stalker.

Wait. *Am* I a weird internet stalker?

"It's not until April," Sutton tells me. "But the National Championship Fly is only three and a half weeks away."

"The National Championship Fly?"

"It's an NBRC thing. The National Birmingham Roller Club," she explains. "It's kind of a big deal. Dad thinks we might even be able to place in the Regionals. There's not a lot of people who fly around here."

I'm just opening my mouth to ask Sutton how they shipped the pigeons all the way from Washington, DC, when I hear a strange, low-pitched trilling noise. I've never heard anything like it before. Kind of like an old-fashioned telephone (a *really* old one, not just our landline), but muffled with a pillow.

I look up.

The kit is circling lower and lower, a few of the birds almost grazing the top of the shed with their wings. I tense as I'm surrounded by birds. I was expecting them to glide smoothly down to the little landing platform just inside the coop's door, like planes on a runway, but they come in fast, awkwardly flapping their wings as they bank hard above the coop, first one way, and then another.

Sutton steps forward, shooing the birds inside with a practiced flick of her hands. As the last bird stumbles to a stop on the platform, she scoops it up. Cradling her hands together, she uses her fingers to support its weight, trapping its feet still between her middle and ring fingers, and pinning its wings to its back with her thumbs.

"Do you want to hold it?" She thrusts the pigeon in my direction.

I swallow.

Up close, the pigeon is smaller than I'd expected, a banana with feathers. Its head and tail are white, and its body is a hodgepodge of pale gray and white.

It moves constantly, struggling to work its way out of Sutton's grasp. Its hood-shaped head twists nearly all the way around, like a tiny *Exorcist* pigeon. Two small, perfectly black, perfectly round eyes are positioned on either side of its head.

Between Sutton's fingers, its pink, pronged feet are gnarly-looking. They could probably do some damage, if they wanted to.

"Um . . ." I swallow again. "Maybe I could just look at it?"

"Sure. Here." Twisting her hand to accommodate the new grip, Sutton reaches out and spreads the pigeon's wing, opening it as wide as she can. "It's pretty, right?" Sutton asks. "It's a lavender bald head."

The pigeon blinks up at me as I lean closer. Its neck feathers catch the sun, glinting purple, and teal, and green in the light. Like a prism, I think randomly. "Is it okay if I touch it?" I ask, surprising myself.

"Yeah, of course." She holds the bird closer.

I reach out. For a second, I think the pigeon is going

to peck at me with its beak, but it burrows its head into Sutton's hand instead. I stroke the back of its neck, just barely brushing the feathers with the tips of my fingers.

The feathers are soft. Really soft. Like the silk table-cloth Mom uses for Christmas, or when we have fancy company for dinner.

I've never touched a bird before. We don't have any pets, because Mom and Dad think I'm not ready for the responsibility yet. If we ever do get one, I'm sure it'll be something normal, like a dog or a cat. Do people even have birds as pets anymore?

The pigeon is quivering beneath my finger. It seems weird that it can be so freaked out by somebody touching its neck when, ten minutes ago, it was doing kamikaze backflips a mile up in the air.

I can't help wondering what it feels like to go for it like that. To just throw yourself backward through the air and *roll*.

I jump a little as Sutton's phone chimes, drawing away from the bird. Thrusting it into the coop, she pulls her cell out, making a face as she reads the text.

"My mom. She's big on eating breakfast together."

"What time is it?" I ask. Sutton holds up her phone for me to see.

Seven fifteen. I should get back before Mom leaves for work.

"I'm going to head out," I say. "Um, thanks for showing me the coop, though. And you know, the bird, and . . . everything. It was cool."

There's an awkward pause for a second, but neither of us move to go.

"Yeah, well." Sutton twines a strand of bright red hair between her fingers. I think I'm finally starting to get used to the color. "I'm out here most mornings, if you ever get bored."

"Okay," I say. "Thanks."

As I head down the driveway toward home, I wonder if Sutton and I are friends now.

I hope so.

CHAPTER 8

MOM DOESN'T EVEN seem to notice how long I've been gone on my "run." A quick smile, an even quicker kiss on the top of my head (which I do my best to dodge), and she's out the door. I'm just about to grab a soda when her head pops back in.

"Aiden's dad is dropping him off, right?"

I'd almost forgotten about Aiden coming over. "Yeah," I tell Mom. "And his mom is going to take us to Three Men on her lunch break."

"Okay. You two behave. Good run?"

I nod, feeling guilty. Mom smiles. Her front tooth sticks out just the tiniest bit. Not mine; perfect teeth, Dr. Sawyer says. I'm a meticulous flosser.

After Mom leaves, I take a quick shower and then watch a couple of old episodes of *Bananaman* online. They're not as good as the comic book, but they're still pretty great. Especially the Nerks, these green, slimy aliens who are working with General Blight to take over the world.

Aiden and I used to have this joke about the popular kids being Nerks who were trying to take over Westville. Only instead of laser blasters, they had iPhones.

Mr. Sorenson drops Aiden off at nine, giving me his signature double honk and driver's window wave. I wave back as Aiden gets out of the car, hitching a backpack up on his shoulder.

"What's in the bag?" I push open the world's noisiest screen door, holding it for Aiden.

He shrugs. "Just some stuff. Oh, and my mom sent cookies."

Mrs. Sorenson makes the most awesome chocolate chip cookies I've ever had. Even *my* mom admits they're the best.

"Excellent," I say, rubbing my hands together in anticipation.

Aiden grins. "You look like a supervillain."

"The Chocolate Chip Menace," I say, dropping my voice as low as it will go. Which isn't very low.

"You might want to work on that," Aiden observes.

He pulls a Tupperware container out of his backpack, hands it to me, and then tosses the bag onto the couch. "So anyway, my mom said she'll be here around eleven."

I pry open the cover of the Tupperware. The sweet, sweet aroma of freshly baked chocolate chip cookies floods the air.

Seriously. They're the best.

"Cool," I tell Aiden. Stuffing an entire cookie in my mouth, I lead the way toward the basement. "That means another ten bucks each to spend at Three Men."

Aiden follows me down the stairs. "Speaking of which, did you hear about the new Marvel casting? There's no way he's going to get the Gambit accent right. . . ."

← ← ← ← ← ←

An hour and a half later, Aiden and I have discussed the following things: whether or not anyone can actually pull off a Cajun accent (I voted no), how much puke a human body can hold (a lot), and how many teachers secretly pick their noses when they think no one is looking (at least three that we can think of).

We've also sorted through about six tons of accumulated junk, including three boxes full of jam jars, a stack of *National Geographic* magazines from the mid-2000s, a suitcase stuffed with old winter coats, and fourteen empty kitty litter containers.

"What's in here?" Aiden asks, grunting a little as he drags a large cardboard box into the center of the floor. "It's heavy."

Marking the article on earthquakes that I'm reading, I set the *National Geographic* aside and join Aiden. There's a thick coating of dust on top of the box, and we both cough a little as he pulls open the flaps.

"Whoa," he says, peering down into the box. "What, did your grandma rob a trophy store?"

I reach inside, pulling out the tallest trophy. It's so big that I have to use both hands. "Graham Hall," I read aloud. "1986 Minnesota State Runner-up, Boys 3200 Meters."

Aiden pulls another trophy out of the box, brushing the bottom of it off with his shirt. "This one's for the Boys 1600 Meters." His eyes widen a little as he reads the next line. "Four minutes and ten seconds? Are you serious? Your dad ran a mile in *four minutes*? That's impossible!"

I set the trophy I'm holding down before I drop it.

"I guess so," I say, trying not to think about how long it takes me to run a mile. When I manage to make it a mile without stopping, that is.

"Impossible," Aiden repeats, grinning. "He's like The Flash."

Only Dad doesn't even know who The Flash is. He

was asking me about him one time, and he called him The Flasher.

"There's got to be, like, two dozen of these," Aiden says, digging through the trophy box. "Hey, did you know your dad did long jump, too?" he asks, holding up a fake-gold medal strung on a red, white, and blue ribbon. "Twenty-one feet."

Twenty-one feet. That's almost five times as tall as I am.

I'm feeling a little sick all of a sudden. I probably had too many of Mrs. Sorenson's cookies. Or maybe it was the Oreos.

"And look, some of these are even from college," Aiden says. "The Badgers, wherever they're from."

"Wisconsin," I say. "He went to college in Wisconsin."

"Ah. The Land of Cheese," Aiden says wisely.

I manage a smile, somehow. "Anyway, we should probably call it a day," I say. "Won't your mom be here soon?"

Aiden pulls out his phone to check. "Oh, yeah. I'm going to go change quick, okay? Just in case we run into anyone."

I stare after him in confusion as he heads for the steps. Who would we possibly run into at Three Men and a Comic Book? Honestly, I don't know how Mike even manages to stay in business; it always seems like Aiden and I are the only ones there.

As he disappears up the stairs, I pack the trophies back into their box, doing my best not to read the other plaques.

Something tells me I don't want to know what they say.

CHAPTER 9

MRS. SORENSON DRIVES really, really slowly up our driveway, making sure not to kick up any dust on her pristine Mercedes SUV.

As I climb in the car, I notice that the shirt Aiden's changed into is new. Which sounds like a creepy thing to say, but until we moved earlier this summer, I spent almost every day with him. Sadly, I know his wardrobe like the back of my hand.

Which is kind of a weird expression, when you think about it. After all, who's just sitting around, staring at the backs of their hands?

Anyway, Aiden's shirt is pretty memorable; a pale blue, short-sleeved button-down covered with tiny dolphins.

It's . . . interesting.

Especially since, like me, 99 percent of his usual wardrobe consists of comic book T-shirts. I'm wearing my old Green Hornet one today. Even though it's a small, it's about two sizes too big for me.

"New shirt?" I ask Aiden.

He shrugs. "Yeah. I grew again."

Now that I think about it, Aiden *does* look bigger. His knees are almost touching the back of his mom's seat, and his shoulders kind of stick straight out, instead of sloping down like they used to. Even his elbows look bigger.

My Green Hornet shirt would probably fit him perfectly.

"Dolphins," I observe. "I didn't know you were into dolphins."

He looks confused. "What are you talking about?"

"Your shirt," I say, gesturing toward his chest.

Aiden looks down, then shrugs. "It's just a shirt," he says.

I nod.

He's right, I guess.

Fifteen minutes later, Mrs. Sorenson pulls up in front of Three Men, leaving the SUV idling. "Don't worry, I won't come in and embarrass you. Twenty minutes, okay? I have to get back to work soon."

"Fine," Aiden says.

"Okay, Mrs. Sorenson," I say, unbuckling my seat belt. "Thanks for taking us."

She smiles at me in the rearview mirror. "Have fun."

I open the door and hop out of the car. Literally. The SUV is so far off the ground that my legs can't reach.

I hate being short.

Much like the faded, blue-and-white-striped awning outside, the rest of Mike's store has seen better days, too. The buzzing fluorescent lights only make it easier to see the stains on the carpet, the cashier's counter is littered with disposable coffee cups, and it's always freezing in the winter, because Mike's worried about the heating bill.

Mom says Three Men lacks "a woman's touch."

Anyway, I don't have a problem with the way Three Men looks. After all, Mike isn't selling accessories. He's selling comics.

And he has them all.

Row after row of display shelves line the walls, all of them stuffed full. There are your standard superhero comics, like *Batman*, *Superman*, *Captain America*, etc. Sci-fi ones, like *eXistenZ* or *Orbiter*. Tons of manga, then fantasy, crime, autobiographical, *fumetti neri* . . .

Let's just say if they make it, Mike's got it.

Or he can order it for you.

The tiny bell over the door gives a strangled ring as we push our way inside. As usual, the door sticks a little in the humidity. Mike's chair behind the counter is empty. Twenty bucks says he's in back, microwaving his lunch.

I take a breath, inhaling deeply. "Chicken pot pie," I tell Aiden. "Definitely."

Aiden and I have a standing competition called "Guess That Odor!" when it comes to Mike's lunch. It started last summer, when Mike was going through his "Make-His-Own-Kimchee" phase.

I looked it up, and kimchee is basically fermented cabbage.

Let me repeat that. *Fermented cabbage.*

It was . . . unpleasant.

Aiden gives the air a sniff as I head for the bargain bin of comics sitting against the far wall. You can find some awesome stuff hidden in there, if you look hard enough. Especially since not a lot of kids tend to like the same stuff I do. Basically, if it's not written between 1956 and 1970, I'm not interested. Except for *Banana-man,* of course, but even that's a throwback to the Silver Age.

"I don't know," Aiden says. His phone chimes in his pocket. He pulls it out, grinning a little as he reads the message. "Soup?"

"Soup?" I repeat. "That's the best you can do?"

He doesn't look up as he taps out a message in reply.

"Come on," I coax. "You didn't even guess what *kind* of soup." I flip through the half-price comics, pretending to read the issue numbers.

Aiden slides his phone back into his pocket. "Chicken noodle?"

To be fair, the odor wafting its way beneath the door is distinctly chicken-y. But I can tell he isn't trying.

"Who's texting you?" I ask, trying not to let my voice sound weird. My fingers are flipping faster through the comics now. *Power Girl. Original Sin. Daredevil.*

"Just Kurt." Aiden isn't purposefully not looking at me, but he's *not* purposefully not looking at me, either.

"Kurt," I repeat. "What's old Kurt up to today?" I ask. *Old Kurt?* What am I talking about? Have I somehow turned into Dad without realizing it?

"Nothing." Aiden feigns interest in the latest *Walking Dead* issue. "Just checking in." Aiden doesn't like *The Walking Dead*. He's strictly Marvel. *X-Men*, to be exact. I think he has a thing for Jean Grey. Anyway, he thinks the zombie apocalypse is played out.

I flip past another *Daredevil*. "Checking in?" Flip. *Captain America.* "You guys check in with each other now?"

"I don't know. Kind of." Aiden's eyes dart toward

me for a second, then away. "He's trying to talk me into going out for basketball with him."

Flip, flip, flip. I'm not even looking at the comics now.

"But you don't even play basketball," I say.

"I didn't *used* to. But I'm tall now. Maybe I'll be good at it."

"You don't know that," I argue. "Correlation does not imply causation. Don't you remember science class?"

Aiden shoots me an annoyed look. Science has never been his best subject. He didn't even want to join the Arduino Challenge team last year, even though it meant a whole day off school for the competition. In the end, it was just Sarah Stockdale and me.

We placed second, by the way.

"Yeah, well, not all of us are as into science as you are," Aiden says. "Anyway, what's the big deal? You're going out for cross-country, but you don't see me freaking out about it."

"But you don't even like basketball," I say. "You told me any sport where you have to wear a tank top isn't worth it."

Aiden shrugs. "Yeah, well . . . Things change, I guess. Hey, look, they have the new *X-Men*. Awesome."

Things change.

And just like that, standing in the hot, vaguely chicken-y smelling front room of Three Men and a Comic, I feel something in our friendship shift.

Something big.

Flip.

CHAPTER 10

I FALL ASLEEP to *Bananaman* episodes that night, my laptop balanced on my nightstand.

A familiar knocking sound wakes me.

"Ren?"

I groan, opening my eyes just a crack. It's still dark. Why is Dad waking me up when it's still dark?

"Can I come in?" Dad calls through the door.

I turn to look out the window.

No wonder it still seems like the middle of the night; thick, black thunderclouds crowd against one another, darkening the early-morning sky. It isn't raining yet, but I can see the wind whipping through the tree branches, shaking the leaves like giant pom-poms.

I'm not seriously supposed to run in this, am I?

"It's going to *thunderstorm*," I call back. "Do you *want* me to be struck by lightning?"

Dad opens the door. "Yes. I want my only son to be struck by lightning. How did you guess?"

"Ha ha."

He grins. "It's not supposed to rain until seven, by the way. I'm heading out, but I wanted to let you know Mom got called in early, so you didn't worry." His expression turns serious. "Don't think I haven't noticed how hard you've been working lately, kiddo. Now that you're putting the effort in, your totals are really starting to shape up. I'm proud of you. You deserve a day off."

I shift uncomfortably in bed, not quite meeting his eye.

I drew a straight line on my chart yesterday, even though I'd only run half a mile.

I've never done that before. I've never *cheated*.

"Anyway," Dad says, tapping the door with his fingers. "I've gotta run, but I'll see you this afternoon."

I mumble something unintelligible, then pull the blankets over my head.

As the door clicks shut behind him, I stay hidden beneath the covers, breathing shallowly. I'm not going to lie; it's a little musky under here. I should probably get around to washing my sheets.

I emerge from my cave, settling my head back into the pillow. Closing my eyes, I lie there and wait to fall back asleep.

And wait.

And wait.

It's no good. How am I supposed to sleep when I'm feeling so guilty?

Kicking back my covers, I dig through my hamper for clean-ish running clothes.

If I hurry, I can make it down in time for Dad to see me.

⤝ ⤝ ⤝ ⤝ ⤝ ⤝

Ten minutes later, I'm cursing the fact I didn't stay in bed.

Despite Dad's promise that it would hold off, a cold rain is starting to fall, making it hard to see. Why don't they make windshield wipers for your glasses?

I make a mental note to add that to my list of inventions. Someday, when I'm old enough to file a patent, I'm going to be rich.

By the time I reach Sutton's driveway, I'm breathing heavily, and my right side is starting to throb again. I ball my fist to my hip, trying to "run through the pain" like one of Dad's running shirts says.

It's no good.

I don't want to run through the pain.

I want to stop.

The rain is growing heavier. The wind picks up, gusting cold sheets of water over my head.

Sheets. Yet another reminder to do my laundry.

I eye the trees lining the driveway, trying to calculate the risk of being killed by a falling branch. Deciding I like my odds, I head for their relative shelter.

Taking off my glasses, I wipe them with the bottom of my shirt.

Excellent. Now they're wet *and* smeary.

As I put my glasses back on, I can just make out a blurry shape hurrying down the steps of Sutton's house.

A second later, I hear the sound of an engine turning over. The red station wagon pulls out, making its way down the driveway.

I fight the urge to duck behind a tree trunk and hide. The car slows to a stop in front of me, and a lady who must be Sutton's mom lowers her window. "Hi, there! Everything okay?"

Even with my smeary glasses, I can tell that Sutton's mom doesn't look old enough to be a mom. Her blonde hair is long and wavy, and she's wearing a lot of eye makeup for six thirty in the morning.

"Sorry. I got a side ache, and it started raining, so . . ." I trail off.

"You must be Lauren. That's quite a name."

"Yep," I agree. "Quite a name."

She gives me a bright smile. "Sutton mentioned you'd stopped by before. I'm Eva. It's so nice to meet you!"

"Oh. Thanks," I say awkwardly. "Nice to meet you, too."

"I've been meaning to stop by and welcome you to the neighborhood, but you know how it is." She gives a little laugh.

I clear my throat. "That's okay. We just moved from town, so it's not like we're new, or anything."

"Can I give you a ride?" Sutton's mom asks. "I'm heading in that direction. Or you know what?" she says, brightening. "Why don't you just go inside the house? I have to get to the hospital, but I made a huge breakfast. Sutton could use some help eating it all."

I can't help wondering what the inside of Sutton's house looks like.

Also, breakfast.

"Are you sure?" I ask.

"Of course! I've got to run, but head right in." She smiles, shooing me toward the house as she rolls up her window.

When I get to the steps, though, I hesitate. Am I really going to knock on Sutton's door? Just like that? Out of nowhere?

A burst of rain answers my question for me. Ducking

my head, I take the steps two at a time.

Raising my hand, I knock, quietly at first, and then, as another gust of rain drenches me, louder. "Sutton? Are you in there? It's Ren."

A second later, Sutton pulls open the door. She looks confused. "Hey. What are you doing here? I'm not flying today."

"No, I know," I say quickly. "I was out running, and it started to rain, and your mom saw me . . ."

Sutton's face clears in understanding. "Let me guess. She told you I needed help eating all the food she made." Pushing the screen door open, she lets me in.

"Thanks."

I step inside, dripping water, and do my best to look around without being too obvious about it. The layout of Sutton's house is familiar: same narrow entrance hall, same steep wooden steps, same stained glass insert over the kitchen door. But whereas our house is meticulously neat, with fresh flowers on the hall table and embarrassing yearbook photos of me already lining the walls, Sutton's house is . . . not.

Not like it's *dirty*, or anything; the floor looks clean enough. But there are piles of . . . stuff . . . everywhere. Stacks of folded laundry sit on the steps, a heap of magazines overflows the side table, and a box full of cookie cutters sits in the middle of the hallway. Even though they've technically been here longer than us, their walls are still bare, and the only decoration I can see is a takeout menu from Arriba, the local Mexican restaurant, pinned to the corkboard next to the door.

"I'll get you a towel," Sutton says. She eyes me dubiously. "Do you want something of my dad's to wear?"

I kind of don't. Whatever she chooses, it's bound to be huge on me, and I'll look ridiculous.

Still, ridiculous is better than cold and wet.

Well, maybe.

"Thanks," I say aloud.

"I'll be right back," she says, pounding up the stairs. "I hope you like French toast!"

CHAPTER 11

THERE'S A MASSIVE amount of French toast in Sutton's kitchen.

The plate on the table must be piled at least a foot high with slices of golden-brown bread. Next to the plate sits a bowl of strawberries and another bowl full of homemade whipped cream.

I've never even seen homemade whipped cream before.

"Wow."

"I told you." Sutton shrugs.

"But there's got to be an entire loaf of bread there."

"Yep." Sutton stands on her tiptoes, grabbing plates from the frosted glass cupboard. She hands one to me, then pulls open the silverware drawer. All the knives and forks and spoons are jumbled together in a big heap.

The rest of the kitchen resembles the hallway; half-emptied boxes sit on the counter, hand towels are draped across chair backs, and the coffeemaker is balanced precariously on top of the bread box.

"We can eat in my bedroom," Sutton says quickly, catching my expression. "We're still getting set up down here. My dad's the organized one."

"How's he doing?" I ask awkwardly.

Sutton loads three slices of toast onto her plate. "Good. He's starting rehab this week."

"Oh. Cool." I take a couple of pieces of bread, piling them high with strawberries and whipped cream.

"So do you want to watch a movie, or something?" Sutton asks.

"Sure." Carefully balancing my plate, I follow Sutton up the stairs. The plain white T-shirt she found for me (straight out of the package, thankfully, with creases and everything) is predictably huge on me. You can't even see my shorts.

Have I mentioned that I hate being short?

I pause awkwardly in the doorway, my plate clutched to my chest.

I've never been in a girl's room before.

Or at least, not for years. Not since it counted.

Sutton's room is the complete opposite of the chaos downstairs. Her bed is made, the top of her dresser is bare, and the only things on her nightstand are a box of Kleenex and an alarm clock. The walls are a deep, rich color that Mom would probably call "eggplant" and Dad would call "purple." Framed movie posters hang on three of them, old, black-and-white films I don't recognize. The fourth wall, behind her bed, is completely covered with a huge photo collage.

It smells nice.

Like the bathroom in Dr. Sawyer's dental office. Which isn't as weird as it sounds; trust me, it's a *really* nice bathroom.

If Sutton feels at all weird about having a boy in her room, she doesn't show it. She flops down on the floor and stuffs a huge bite of French toast into her mouth, smearing whipped cream on her chin.

Stepping inside, I look at the nearest photo. Sutton is posed at the edge of a lake with a man that has to be her father. He looks even younger than her mom. "Your parents are really young," I say, immediately kicking myself. Is it rude to talk about how old someone's parents are? Mom would know.

"Yeah, they got married in college, after Mom got knocked up with me," Sutton says matter-of-factly. "I was a total surprise baby."

I blink. "Oh. I was a surprise baby, too. Only kind of the opposite. My parents are really old. Well, not *really* old," I clarify. "Statistically, though, they're older than the average parents."

Sutton wipes whipped cream from her chin with the back of her hand, then licks it. "That's cool. I bet you get away with a lot of stuff."

I'm too embarrassed to admit the only thing I've ever "gotten away with" is not reminding Mom the summer she forgot to sign me up for swimming lessons. And in the end that backfired on me; the next summer, I was the only fifth grader in the fourth grade class.

Which is why I still hold my nose when I jump in a pool.

Anxious to change the subject, I peer at the rest of the photos. There are a few of Sutton and her parents stuck around the edges, but the actual collage itself is made up of pictures with Sutton and her friends: their arms wrapped around one another as they stick their tongues out at the camera, dancing at a concert together, screaming as they run through a sprinkler. In the center of the collage, a patch of bright green poster board reads, "We'll Miss You, Sutton!" in sparkly blue letters. Signatures and scribbled notes crowd around the message, taking up every spare inch of space.

Sutton points toward a corner of the collage. "See

that picture, where we're dancing? We snuck into a show in Foggy Bottom to see this band, Lyceum. It was awesome." She wrinkles her nose. "Well, until we got kicked out. Mom and Dad were cool about it, though. I think they were jealous they didn't get to see them."

She gestures toward another picture with her fork. "And see that one, the one that's all blurry? My friend Sarah and I were at the National Portrait Gallery, and we started giving tours to people. Just, like, making stuff up. It was so funny. We ended up having to run away from this security guard. Carl." Sutton grins at the memory.

I stare at the photo, slightly fascinated. "Westville doesn't even have a museum. Unless you count the one in Rochester about the history of Olmsted County. They have a lot of quilts."

Sutton pauses with her fork halfway to her mouth. "Yeah. No offense to Olmsted County, but it's not really the same thing."

She has a point. Suddenly, I feel guilty for making such a big deal about moving eight miles away from our old house. Sutton's friends are eight *hours* away. Probably more. I'd have to look it up to find the exact distance.

Either way, it's a lot farther than the ride to Aiden's house.

"Hey," I hear myself saying aloud. "Do you want to come over for dinner tonight? My dad's supposed to grill, if it stops raining. He's kind of terrible at it, but . . ."

"Really?" Sutton asks eagerly. "I mean . . . Yeah. That sounds good. If your parents don't mind."

"They won't," I say confidently. "But, um, just one thing. Do you mind not telling my dad I hung with you yesterday morning? He thinks I was running."

"No problem." Sutton pretends to zip her lips shut and toss the key over her shoulder.

I smile in relief.

Sutton stabs another huge bite of French toast. "So are we watching a movie, or what?"

CHAPTER 12

IT DOESN'T STOP raining.

From the living room window, I can see Sutton and her mom pull their sweatshirts over their heads as they make a break toward the house. Mom is waiting in the hall to open the door.

She's been waiting there for a while now, actually.

It's possible she and Dad were a little too happy when I told them I'd invited our new neighbor over for dinner. I swear, Mom actually squeaked with excitement when I said the word "girl."

"Hello!" At least Mom's voice sounds normal. Well, normal-ish. "You must be Sutton. And Eva, it's so nice to meet you! I'm Audrey Hall. Come in, come in. It's raining cats and dogs out there. I should know; I'm a vet."

I hover in the living room doorway, wincing as they laugh politely at Mom's "joke." Sutton pushes back her hood, her atomic fireball hair catching the overhead light. Mom's eyes widen slightly, but to her credit, she doesn't say anything.

It's weird how sometimes, out of nowhere, you remember that you kind of love your parents.

"Ren told us about your husband," Mom says to Sutton's mom. "I'm so sorry, what a terrible thing to happen."

Sutton's mom's smile doesn't even waver. "Well, things could have been worse," she says brightly. "And Luke's a trouper, luckily."

"Here," I say, reaching out for Sutton's wet hoodie. "Let me take your jacket." I don't know where the words come from. They don't seem like something I'd say in real life. I feel like an actor in a play as I hang the sweatshirt from one of the pegs on the wall.

"I was telling Lauren, I've been meaning to get over and welcome you," Sutton's mom says, pushing her wet bangs out of her eyes. "But you know how it is."

Dad pops his head out of the kitchen, holding a spatula. "Hello!" he says. "You must be Sutton and Eva. Can we talk you into staying for dinner, Eva?"

Sutton's mom smiles apologetically. Despite the rain, her eye makeup looks perfect. She must use the waterproof kind.

"That's so nice of you. I can't tonight, but thank you so much for having Sutton. It's been hard meeting friends since we moved."

"*Mom.*" Sutton flicks a meaningful gaze in her direction. Eva rolls her eyes, waving her away.

"Sorry, sorry. I'm being the embarrassing mom, aren't I?" She reaches out to wrap her arm around Sutton, but Sutton wriggles away. "All right," Eva says in exasperation. She shares a look with Mom and Dad.

Sutton rolls her eyes at me. She looks just like her mom.

"I'll be back at eight, if that's okay?" Eva looks to Mom for confirmation.

"Of course. Can we drop her off for you?"

"I'll be swinging back from town anyway. But thank you again. Have fun, sweetheart!" With a final smile, Sutton's mom pulls her sweatshirt back over her head and scurries out to her car.

"So, Sutton," Dad asks, leaning against the door frame. He flips the spatula from one hand to another. Casual mode. "How are you liking Westville? Ren said you were from DC? I'm Graham, by the way," he goes on, not waiting for answers. "And yes, I know what you're thinking." He points the spatula in her direction. "It *is* like the cracker."

Sutton gives him a hesitant smile while a small part of me dies from embarrassment.

"Now, are you going to want a real burger, or should I get one of Audrey's fake food ones out of the freezer for you?" Dad asks.

"It's not fake *food*, it's fake meat," Mom says.

"A real burger would be great. Thanks."

Dad grins. "I like her already," he stage-whispers, leaning toward Mom. Sutton's smile widens. I can see her shoulders relaxing.

"Um, do you want to see my room?" I ask. "Or we could hang out in the living room, too."

"I could see your room." Sutton shrugs. She gives Mom and Dad a little wave. "Nice to meet you."

"Dinner's in ten minutes," Dad calls up the stairs after us. "I'm making my famous mashed potatoes!"

"He adds cheese," I explain, opening the door to my room. "I don't know why he thinks that makes them famous."

As I step inside, my stomach gives a nervous flip. I spent the afternoon cleaning, but there's always the chance an odor may be lingering and I just can't smell it.

I can feel my back stiffening as Sutton looks around

my room. Thankfully, I haven't unpacked too much yet, so there isn't a lot of embarrassing evidence lying around. In fact, aside from my comic books, the room is pretty much bare. Even my posters are all still rolled up, since I haven't decided what color to paint the walls yet.

It feels strange, having someone besides Aiden in my room. Like Sutton is peeking into my diary, or something.

Not that I have a diary. But you get what I mean.

"Whoa," Sutton says, pointing toward the top of my dresser. "What's that?"

I follow her finger. "Oh. Um, that's my handheld VDG. Van de Graaff generator," I clarify. "It was my entry for the science fair last year." Aiden and I were supposed to do it together, but he got bored halfway into it. He ended up expanding gummy bears in different liquids instead.

To the casual observer, it kind of just looks like a piece of PVC pipe with a couple of wires running out of it stuck to a soda can, but it was actually really hard to make. The bottom roller was the trickiest part. I tried Teflon tape and silicon rubber, but it turned out that polyvinyl chloride electrical tape worked the best.

"What does it do?" Sutton asks, picking it up curiously.

"It's a static generator," I explain. "You generate a negative charge, and you can kind of make things . . . float. You probably don't want to turn it on," I warn hastily as Sutton's finger hesitates above the motor. "If you have your cell phone with you, it might . . . kill it."

Sutton quickly sets the VDG down. "Last year my dad and I made a battery out of a potato for my science fair project. Hey, did I tell you about his bone graft? My dad's? His doctor says he's the fastest healer he's ever seen."

"That's awesome," I say. "So did you use one of those kits? For the potato? Or did you make everything yourself?"

Sutton shrugs. "Just a kit." Turning toward my night-stand, she plucks a small, plastic trophy from the box of school stuff sitting on top of it.

I can feel myself flushing in embarrassment. What was I thinking, leaving that out? She probably thinks I'm some sort of egotistical monster now.

"That's nothing," I say. "Really."

I can't help thinking about the giant cardboard box sitting in the middle of the basement. The one stuffed to the brim with Dad's trophies. Real ones, made of actual metal. The ones he earned for doing real, actual, trophy-worthy things.

"First Place, Olmsted County Mathlete Competition," Sutton reads. "The Mathletes? Is that, like, the school's Math Club?"

"Ignore that," I say, grabbing the trophy. "The name's supposed to be a joke. Like an athlete? Only with math?"

Sutton snorts.

I shove the trophy back in the box. "I know. It's a pretty terrible joke."

"No, it's funny. Math is cool. Like astronomy? When you think about it, it's all just math."

Math is cool? I give Sutton a dubious look. Still, it doesn't seem like she's making fun of me.

"Whoa." Sutton's eyes widen as she catches sight of my bookshelf.

Well, bookshelves.

"Are those all comics?" she asks. Forgetting the trophies, she wades deeper into my room. Crouching down, she reads off some of the titles. "*Captain Atom, The Flash, Fighting American, Nature Boy* . . . I haven't even heard of half of these." She pulls a comic off the lower shelf. "*Bananaman*?"

"Uh, yeah." She's holding up one of the earlier issues, back when it was still printed in *Nutty*.

Sutton is flipping through the pages. "'The ancient art of Gub Fu'? 'Atomic water pistol'?" she asks. "This looks great. Can I borrow it?"

"Um . . ." Normally, I don't like to lend my comics out to people unless I know I can trust them, like Aiden. On the other hand, no one but Aiden has ever asked. "Yeah. I mean, as long as you're, you know . . . careful . . ." I make a weird little flourish with my hands. "Be my guest."

Great. I'm the teapot from *Beauty and the Beast*.

Not that I would ever admit to having seen *Beauty and the Beast*.

"Awesome. I'll take good care of it," Sutton promises. She carefully sets the *Bananaman* down on top of the nearest box. "So how come you haven't unpacked yet?"

It's a good question.

There's probably a psychological reason. Like, if I unpack my boxes, I'll have to admit the move is permanent.

Or maybe I'm just lazy.

"I'm still deciding what color I want to paint," I tell Sutton.

She surveys the walls. They're a weird sort of peach color, leftover from when my room used to be Aunt Lucy's. "It does kind of look like Barbie threw up in here."

"Stomach Flu Barbie," I joke in my best television

presenter voice. "Now accessorized with her very own bucket."

She laughs. "So what color are you going for?"

"I don't know. I want red, but my mom says the room is too small. She thinks it would be like living in a tomato." I'm not about to tell her the reason I want the color red is because of the Justice League's Red Room, a secret, underground research facility that holds some of the most dangerous technology in the world.

As Mom would say, not everyone needs to know everything I'm thinking all the time.

Sutton flops down on my bed.

There is a girl on my bed.

I make a mental note to tell Aiden later.

"You should definitely paint it red. That would look awesome."

"Yeah. Maybe." I mean, it's my room, isn't it? I'm the one who has to live in it. What if I *want* to live in a tomato?

"I could help you, if you want," Sutton offers. "I painted my room myself when we moved. I'm pretty good at it."

"Yeah, maybe," I repeat. "Thanks."

"Kids?" Dad calls up the stairs. "Dinner's ready. Come and get it before Audrey eats it all!"

Sutton pushes herself off the bed.

My bed.

"I like your parents," she says. "Your dad's funny. He seems cool." It takes me a minute to realize Sutton isn't joking. "Hey, can I use your bathroom before we eat?" she asks.

"Um, sure. It's right across the hall."

As Sutton disappears through the doorway, I can't help staring after her. First *math* is cool, and then my dad?

Maybe "cool" means something else in DC.

CHAPTER 13

THE NEXT MORNING, I wake up meaning business.

Ever since I met Sutton, I've been slacking. I still feel guilty about the whole "drawing a straight line on my chart when I didn't actually deserve to" thing from a couple of days ago, and with the rain yesterday ruining my run, I need to get back on schedule.

Plus, I can't stop thinking about that box of trophies in the basement.

Dad's trophies.

The real ones.

I'm so fast opening the door that Dad is still mid-knock. Only (his) quick reflexes keep me from taking a meathook to the face. When I head downstairs, I tear open the strawberry-flavored "energy gel" they threw in for free when I bought my new running shoes. To my surprise, I even manage to keep some of it down.

So as Dad's Subaru turns out of the driveway, I start off after him, fully intending on running my whole three miles.

Really, I do.

But as my initial burst of energy begins to fade, I can feel my best intentions slipping away.

The strawberry gel feels weird and slushy in my stomach. In retrospect, I probably shouldn't have eaten something that came packaged in a shoe box.

I try to think about my stride, about pulling myself up from the top of my head and making sure I pump my arms back and forth, but it's impossible to concentrate.

The thing is, I started looking some stuff up on the internet last night.

Some stuff about pigeons, specifically.

You know, getting new pigeons to fly with the rest of the kit isn't as easy as you'd think. They're not just going to swoop away and start rolling, right off the bat. First off, you need to make sure they're hungry before you let them fly. They have to associate the coop with food, so they have a reason to come back. Otherwise, when you release them for the first time, they might just . . . *poof* . . . fly away.

Obviously, I'm sure Sutton already knows this.

But I wonder if she's familiar with Pavlovian conditioning. Back in the day, there was this scientist guy named Ivan Pavlov, and he did this experiment where he'd ring a bell every time he fed these dogs, and pretty soon they started associating the bell with food, and would drool every time he rang it, even if they couldn't see any food.

Anyway, I don't think anyone uses a bell with pigeons, but I did read some articles about whistling in a low tone and shaking a can full of pigeon feed every time the birds are fed. Then you do the same thing when they're starting to return to the coop after a fly, and they'll associate with eating, and come down, and . . .

I'm going to pop over to Sutton's and talk to her.

Just for a minute.

Turning around, I jog quickly back home. Tiptoeing into the house (Mom was up late with an unplanned Labrador C-section), I grab the hard copies of the articles from the printer.

Cutting through the field toward Sutton's house, I mentally rehearse different greetings. I've never been a Boy Scout, but I *do* believe in being prepared. Is "hey" too casual? Or just casual enough?

Either way, I tell myself, it's better than silently

skulking in the tree line.

But when I reach the coop, Sutton isn't even there. Inside the coop, I can hear the low-pitched trill of the pigeons and the scrabbling of their feet against their perches. I head around to the side, trying to peer through the tiny gap that lines the plywood exit door. I can catch flickers of movement, but that's about it.

I step back, disappointed.

And almost trip over the ladder lying in the grass next to the coop.

The birds are still on top of the loft. The new ones. *Squeakers*, Sutton called them.

I check to make sure Sutton isn't coming, then hoist the ladder up from the ground. Staggering slightly, I prop it against the side of the coop. My heart is beating faster than normal, and my palms feel sweaty. How do criminals commit actual crimes without passing out?

Maybe I should wait for Sutton, after all.

Putting my foot on the bottom rung, I start to climb. I'm not great with heights (*acrophobia*, my brain reminds me), but I'm pretty sure I can handle being seven feet off the ground.

As long as I don't look down, that is.

Ha, I think, as my head clears the top of the coop. I was right.

The two-by-two cage sits near the edge of the roof,

close enough for me to reach out and touch, if I want to. Inside, two pigeons turn to look at me curiously.

They don't look noticeably smaller than the one Sutton showed me the other day, but it's hard to tell. The head and tail feathers of the one closest to me are white, while the rest of him is a pale maroon color, with hints of gray underneath. As he bobs nervously around, flecks of sea foam green and purple catch the light on his neck.

Flecks of sea foam green and purple? I probably shouldn't let anyone hear me say that aloud, unless I'm in the mood to get beaten up that day.

Unlike his roommate, the other pigeon doesn't seem nervous. Cocking his head, he stands still, looking at me curiously. Aside from a tiny patch of white on his beak, he's all black, with the same hint of shiny color beneath his neck feathers. He stares at me with his strange round eyes.

"Hey," I say, staring back at him. "I'm Ren."

He cocks his head to the other side, bobbing his neck up and down a couple of times.

As far as greetings go, it's better than mine.

"Nice to meet you, too," I say, leaning forward. "What's your name?"

"NBRC925-40."

For a microsecond, I think the pigeon has actually

answered me. Then I realize his voice sounds a lot like Sutton's.

Uh-oh.

Well, this is embarrassing.

Holding tightly to the ladder, I look over my shoulder. Sutton grins up at me, her eyes shaded by the same, too-big Nationals cap. "Unless you're talking to NBRC925-41, that is," she says.

"I wasn't talking to him," I say sheepishly. "I mean, not *talking*, talking. Just, you know . . . saying hello."

Sutton's grin widens. "If you mean the red one, I call him Squirrel."

"Squirrel?" I turn back to look at the birds. "Why?"

I can see Sutton shrugging in my peripheral vision. "I don't know. He looks kind of squirrelly, don't you think?"

Now that Sutton mentions it, he *does* look a little . . . jumpy. He's still pacing restlessly around the cage, weaving back and forth like a mechanical toy that's wound too tight.

His cage-mate hasn't moved. Actually, I don't think he's even blinked. With an odd feeling of regret, I start down the ladder. Sutton steps back to make room for me.

"What about the black one?" I ask, regaining solid ground. "Does he have a name?"

"Blue."

"His name's Blue?"

"No, his color. It's blue, not black."

I consider this for a second. "I guess that makes sense." Kind of. Although it really *does* look black.

"What are these?" Sutton asks, reaching down to retrieve the printouts I brought with me. "*Imprinting Birmingham Rollers?*" she reads aloud, turning the pages. "*Conditioning Roller Pigeons for Competition?*"

"Oh, um . . ." I clear my throat. "I did a little research last night."

Sutton stares down at the stack of papers, flipping through them with her thumb.

"Or, you know, a lot of research," I admit.

Maybe this was a bad idea. Sutton probably thinks I'm a total jerk. I mean, what am I doing, coming over here with a stack of research? Telling her how she should train *her* birds? Like Googling them has suddenly made me an expert, or something?

I shift my feet awkwardly back and forth. "I'm sorry," I say. "I didn't mean anything by it. I should probably g—"

"Do you have a hat?" Sutton interrupts.

I blink. "A hat?"

"If you're going to help me train the kit, you're going to need a hat."

A tiny rush of excitement pumps through my veins.

"Really? You want me to help you?"

"Yeah. I mean, if you want." Her voice is casual.

I don't need a mirror to know that I'm grinning my face off. "Okay. Yeah. I mean, if you want."

Sutton grins, too. "Cool."

"Cool," I repeat. "And don't worry. I'll find a hat."

CHAPTER 14

THE NEXT MORNING, Sutton eyes me dubiously.

"Camouflage?" she asks. "What, are you a hunter now?"

"Ha ha," I say, self-consciously adjusting my cap. I found it in the back of Dad's closet last night. I think it's from the one and only time he tried to go pheasant hunting.

She reaches up to scratch her nose, hiding a smile behind the palm of her hand. Her nails have been freshly painted, I notice. Black with red stripes. A suspicious snorting sound escapes from her nose. "Sorry," she says, pulling herself together. "It's great. Perfect. So, do you want to do the honors?"

"Are you sure?" I glance at the coop. "I just . . . open the door?"

She raises her eyebrows.

"Right," I say. "Okay. No problem." I open doors every single day of my life. This one's no different.

Well, aside from the flock of birds lurking on the other side.

The door is about a foot square, cut into the side of the coop around eye level. I step forward, lifting the hook that's keeping it shut. Sutton says that some of the fanciers, the ones whose birds are actually worth money, have to padlock their coops at night to keep their kits from being stolen. A good breeding pigeon can go for five hundred bucks, if you find the right person to buy it.

The door falls open, thudding against the side of the coop.

I duck out of the way. It's not that I'm scared, exactly, I'm just . . . cautious.

Maybe a little overly cautious.

It's only a second or two later when the first bird pushes its way through the slim, metal bars that hang like wind chimes from a rod at the top of the exposed opening.

"The bars only swing one way," Sutton explains. "So the birds can push their way out of the coop, but nothing else can get in. You have to prop the bars up when it's time for the kit to come back in."

I know from my research that Sutton's talking about predatory birds, like owls, or hawks, that prey on smaller birds. The fact that there are birds out there that *eat other birds* is pretty creepy, when you think about it.

Sutton tells me she even keeps a pair of cymbals out by the pigeon coop, just in case she ever needs to scare a hawk away.

The heavy thudding of the pigeon's wings takes me by surprise again as it lurches upward, winging into the air.

One by one, the rest of the kit crowds through the opening, eager to make their way out. It's like a miniature tornado of feathers and feet and confusion and sound. In less than a minute, it's over, and the birds are climbing into the sky.

"You don't want them too low," Sutton says. Her voice sounds loud in the sudden silence. "They need enough height to roll. But too high is worse; sometimes entire kits just . . . drift away. Especially the young ones."

I crick my head back, staring up at the birds. They're gaining height now, starting to crisscross back and forth in a pack.

"How long before they start to roll?" I ask.

"It depends. On a good day, it should just be a few

minutes. In competition, you only have five minutes to time in. Otherwise you're disqualified."

"And you get twenty minutes to fly after you time in, right?" Sutton sent me a link to the National Birmingham Roller Club's (or NBRC's) website last night. I've always prided myself on being an excellent student. "What happens if it starts pouring, or something, right in the middle? Is there a rain delay, or something?"

Sutton shakes her head. "We're just out of luck. There's only one judge for the whole region, so he doesn't have time to wait around for anyone."

So after months of training, a few sprinkles can just ruin everything? "That sucks," I say, making a mental note to check the long-range forecast on the national weather service website later.

"Kind of, yeah," Sutton agrees. "Anyway, here." She holds up a little metal tape measure thingy, like the one I saw her using the first time we met. "It's a tally counter," she explains, handing it to me. "It's my dad's, but you can use it until he gets back home. Did I tell you his doctor said he might be out sooner than we thought?" she asks eagerly.

There's a button on the side of the tally counter. I give it a curious click, and the little number on the side of the counter flips over from zero to one. Click, click. Two, three.

"That's awesome. So this is how you count how many times they roll?"

"Yeah." She clears her throat. "I'm warning you, your thumb is going to be killing you by tonight." Sutton points toward her upper shoulders. "Here, too." I tilt my head back again, experimentally. She's right; now that I think about it, it's pretty uncomfortable.

"We should get those weird neck pillows people use at the airport."

Sutton laughs, even though I wasn't really joking.

"Okay. Basic rules," she says. "The whole point is that you want as many birds as possible to roll at the same time. But you also want them to roll for as long as they can each time they do it. Because the longer they roll, the deeper they're going, and the more points you get."

"As long as they don't go too deep, and splat on the ground, right?"

"Right. You also can get bonus points for speed. So the more birds that roll at the same time, and the faster and the deeper they go, the more points you get."

More birds. Faster. Deeper.

Got it.

Well, kind of.

"Cool," Sutton says. "So under twenty feet, it's one point per bird. Twenty to twenty-nine feet, two points.

Three points for anything over thirty feet. You get a bonus point if they break really fast, or roll anything farther than forty-five feet."

I look up at the sky. "But how can you tell how far twenty feet is? And when a bunch of them are rolling at the same time, how do you count them all at once?"

"Practice." Sutton grins.

"Look," she says, pointing toward the kit. A few of them have just pitched backward into a roll. "When they start rolling like that, it's called 'breaking.' So how many points would you get for that break?"

I concentrate on the birds that are already swooping back up to join the rest of the kit. There's three of them, so . . .

"Easy," I say, clicking the tally counter. "Three points."

Sutton raises her eyebrows.

"Not three points?" I ask in confusion. I'm not used to getting the wrong answer. It feels, well . . . *wrong*.

"That was a deep enough roll for two points each," Sutton explains. "Twenty to twenty-nine feet, remember?"

"Right," I say. Clearing my throat in embarrassment, I click the tally counter three more times. Which brings the total up to . . . nine? That can't be right.

Oh, shoot, I forgot to reset it. How do I . . . wait, they're rolling again! And this time there's a lot of them!

My eyes flick back and forth as I try to count. I click frantically, forgetting about the extra points from before. Are there seven of them? Or eight? And are they rolling deeper than the other ones? Shallower? How are you supposed to even tell?

"Sixteen points," Sutton calls, calmly clicking away on her own counter.

Sixteen points total? Or sixteen new points? Sixteen plus nine is twenty-five, minus the three extra points, and *aargh*! They're going again!!!

"Nine points!"

I click desperately at my counter, trying to catch up. When I glance over in Sutton's direction, she grins. "How's it going?"

"Great!" I lie, trying not to panic.

Okay. You can do this, Ren. Just keep calm.

Two-thirds of the kit drops into an impressive roll, tumbling so deep I'm worried they're going to hit the ground.

"Is that a three pointer?" I call out.

"They're on fire today!"

I nod in agreement, even though it isn't exactly a specific answer, when you think about it.

"Fifty-two total!"

I look down at my tally counter. It reads forty-one.

Sidling over, Sutton peers down at my counter. Then she laughs. "Just try watching for now," she advises me. "It takes a while to get the hang of it."

I try not to be offended. I'm not used to it "taking a while" for me to get the hang of something.

Well, most things, I think, looking down at my shiny athletic shorts.

I fully intend on running after this.

Probably.

If it's not too hot by then.

Dropping my hand, I lean my head back. We settle into silence, disturbed only by the clicking of Sutton's tally counter.

It's peaceful out here, in the middle of the field. The air is warm, the insects buzzing past are actually leaving me alone, and the still-wet ground beneath us smells oddly nice.

I'm not sure how long we stand there, staring up at the kit as they somersault through the air together. Probably longer than I think.

Eventually, though, the rolls become fewer and farther between. Sutton glances at her watch.

"They should be coming down soon." She checks

the face of her counter. "Ninety-six!" She looks up at me, her eyes wide with excitement.

"I take it that's good?"

"With a score like that, we could place at Regionals," she says, grinning. "Although there'll only be eleven birds in the actual competition. We'll have to narrow the kit down before then."

I scan the birds, which are circling lower above the coop.

"What about Squirrel?" I ask. "And Crow? Do you think they'll be ready to fly by then?"

Sutton gives me a look. "Crow?"

Oops. "Oh. Um . . . the other squeaker. The black one. I mean the blue one." I pretend to be very interested in a patch of weeds next to my foot. "He just looked like a Crow, to me."

"Crow" is the name of Bananaman's sidekick. He's, wait for it . . . a crow. Unlike Bananaman though, Crow is supersmart.

Once, just after we'd gotten our report cards back, Aiden joked that he was Bananaman, and I was Crow.

I laughed, because I could tell he wanted me to.

And because I didn't know what else to do.

"Crow," Sutton repeats. "I like it."

I look up. "Really?"

"Sure. Now tell me again how this Pavlov stuff works," she says, thrusting one of the feed cans in my direction. She nods toward the coop, where the first member of the kit is banking downward toward the door. "We're on."

CHAPTER 15

I'M A LITTLE bit nervous when Aiden's mom drops him off on Tuesday morning. We haven't really talked since the not-quite-a-fight we had at the comic book store last week.

To be honest, I wasn't even really sure if he was going to show up.

"Hey," I say as he lopes up the driveway. "You're here."

"Yeah. It's Tuesday, right?"

"Right," I say quickly. "I mean, yeah. Anyway, um, my mom says she's going to take a load of stuff to the thrift store in Rochester this weekend, so we're supposed to clear out as much as we can."

"Cool." He follows me into the house.

I can tell Aiden's nervous, too; he keeps fidgeting with the neck of his T-shirt, tugging it back and forth. It's oddly kind of reassuring. Like somehow the fact that we both feel weird makes it not weird anymore.

I cast around for something to talk about. "So, um, did you see *Shield* last night?" I say, leading the way downstairs. It's not my favorite show, but I know Aiden likes it.

He nods. "Yeah. It was okay."

"Did they really have to be stuck on an airplane the whole time?" I ask. "I mean, if they were about to run out of fuel, why wouldn't they have just landed somewhere?"

"It's called a bottle episode," he says, pulling the lightbulb cord.

"A what?"

"A bottle episode. Just the regular cast, only one set . . . TV shows like them because they're cheap. They don't have to pay for other actors, or anything."

Huh. That makes sense, I guess.

"I didn't know that," I tell Aiden.

He shrugs a little. Grabbing a piece of stray newspaper from the floor, he crumples it into a ball and tosses it toward the empty box sitting in the corner. It lands inside with a soft thump.

"Nice shot."

He spreads his arms wide. "What can I say? I'm the best there is at what I do."

I break into a grin. "But what you do best isn't very nice," I say, finishing the Wolverine quote for him.

Aiden grins back at me, then starts pulling boxes out from underneath the staircase. "Ten bucks says there's another dead mouse in one of these."

I stick out my hand. "Deal."

As we both kneel down and open a box, I feel a little blip of relief.

I don't know what I was worrying about, anyway.

"So this is Mickey's, huh?" Sutton asks later that afternoon, looking around dubiously.

She takes a long slurp of her milk shake.

I have to admit, as far as ambience goes, there isn't much.

Mickey's sits at the edge of town, directly off Highway 63. It's your typical drive-in, with a concrete canopy over the parking spaces and big striped umbrellas shading the picnic tables. They serve hot dogs, fries, milk shakes . . . I think you can even get a veggie burger, if you don't mind it tasting like cardboard.

It's a few minutes past two, and the lunchtime crowd is pretty much gone; aside from a couple of cars on the opposite side of the canopy, we're alone. "It's not exactly the fanciest dining establishment," I say.

"They make a good milk shake." Sutton shrugs, taking another drink. "I like the pineapple."

I give a little shudder. Fruit and ice cream should *not* be mixed.

It feels weird to be out in public with Sutton, instead of at her house. Like we're different people, somehow. Only the same.

"Thanks again for coming with me," Sutton says. "You're doing me a huge favor. Running errands with my mom is the worst. She *always* forgets something, and we have to go back to the same store twice."

Sutton called a couple of hours ago, right after Aiden went home for lunch, and asked if I wanted to go into town with her and her mom.

"She should make a list." I take a slurp of my chocolate malt. I always get extra malt powder, just a tiny bit of whipped cream, and no cherries. See above, re: fruit and ice cream.

"She does," Sutton says. "It doesn't help."

"So we're going to let Squirrel and Crow fly with the rest of the kit soon, right?" I ask, changing the subject. "They should have the hang of it by now."

Especially when you consider the fact that Crow is practically a pigeon genius. Like the other day, he pecked my hand after I fed him, and I'd *swear* he was saying thank you. I could almost *hear* him, you know?

Anthropomorphism, my brain whispers. *The attribution of human characteristics to an animal.*

I can't help the fact I'm getting attached to the little guy, though. And the rest of the kit, too, after all the time I've spent with them. Even Squirrel has grown on me . . . in a strange, twitchy sort of way.

My time down at the coop is paying off in more practical ways, too, like how I'm finally getting better at scoring. Sure, my neck and shoulders are constantly sore, there's a weird tan line at the base of my throat from staring up at the kit, and I'm still nowhere near as good as Sutton, but I'm improving.

It helped when I figured out the pigeons seem to roll at a fairly constant rate, between eight and twelve revolutions per second (I borrowed Mom's phone, then slowed the footage down on YouTube. It's easy, if you know what you're doing). So instead of trying to guess how deep they're rolling, I can just measure time instead. One second equals ten revolutions (per average), which equals fifteen feet. Two seconds equals thirty feet, and so on.

I'm still not sure about math being *cool*, but it's definitely helpful.

I also came up with the idea of making a platform for

the birds to land on just outside the coop's door. A piece of plywood, some bracing boards, a couple of nails, and three Band-Aids later, we were in business. After the rest of the kit had headed back inside the coop, Sutton and I scattered some feed onto the platform, then let Squirrel and Crow out of their cage; they ate a few bites, and then we shooed them into the loft with the rest of the birds.

Not to brag, but it worked like a charm.

On a side note, did you know that the peas in pigeon feed mix look exactly like dried boogers? Just in case you were interested.

"Yeah. You're still coming over tonight to fill out the paperwork for the Fly, right?"

"Definitely," I say.

"You know, I've only been in town a few times since we moved," Sutton says, changing the subject again. "I keep expecting it to look like DC. Weird, huh?"

"Kind of. Considering there's, like, seven hundred thousand more people in Washington than there are here." After that first morning at Sutton's house, I looked some stuff up on the internet. Did you know that the Washington Monument is actually two different colors? Apparently they ran out of money halfway through building it.

"Technically, I lived in Arlington. It's a suburb."

"Still bigger than Westville, I bet."

Sutton reaches for one of the fries from the order we're splitting. The great thing about Mickey's is that they always throw a couple of onion rings in, too. My personal theory is that one onion ring is perfect, two are slightly too many, and anything over three is disgusting.

"A little," Sutton agrees. "So what do people do for fun around here?"

"There's the pool. And the bowling alley. And . . ." I trail off, trying to think.

Sutton stares at me. "Two things?" she asks in disbelief. "Seriously? You can't even think of a third?"

"The library!" I say triumphantly, helping myself to a fry. "There's a little lounge, with beanbags and stuff, and they let you bring liquids in, as long as you have a lid."

Sutton drops her head to the table. "I can't believe we live here now," she moans. "No offense."

"It's not too bad. Don't forget about the quilt museum," I joke.

But instead of laughing, Sutton nods her pointy chin over my shoulder. "Do you know that guy? He's looking at you."

I turn to peer at the shiny Jeep station wagon that's just pulled in. Kurt is opening the passenger door, while

Aiden has already piled out of the backseat. Atticus and John are climbing out after him.

I can't help staring. Aiden didn't say anything about hanging out with Kurt today. Why wouldn't he have told me when we were cleaning out the basement this morning?

Aiden's gaze flicks between Sutton and me. I peer over the top of the faded picnic table at Sutton, trying to visualize how we must look to Aiden. Her volcano red hair is twisted into tiny little knots all over her head, and she's wearing combat boots instead of flip-flops.

I'm wearing a Captain America T-shirt and khaki cargo shorts.

Even from here, I can see Aiden's eyes widening.

"Whoa." Kurt steps out of the Jeep, brushing his hair back with the heel of his hand. He gives Sutton and me a casual nod.

Everything Kurt does is casual.

I told you he was cool.

Atticus and John, on the other hand, are openly gawking at Sutton, nudging each other back and forth with their elbows as they stare.

Kurt leans back in the Jeep to say something to his mom, then walks toward our table. Aiden, Atticus, and John follow.

"Hey, man," Kurt says, giving me a friendly nod. Or

at least I think it's friendly. "Good to see you."

I clear my throat. "Um," I say. "Yes. Good to see you, too."

"Who's this?" he asks, looking in Sutton's direction.

Sutton answers for herself. "This is Sutton." Her shoulders are stiff as she raises her milk shake to take a drink. "Who are you?"

Kurt gives her an easy grin, flicking his hair back again. "I'm Kurt. And that's John, Atticus, and Aiden," he says, pointing in their directions.

"Oh." Sutton's shoulders relax just a little bit. "Ren's friend, right?" she asks, looking at Aiden. Is it my imagination, or does he shoot a look in Kurt's direction before he answers her with a nod?

"Sutton's new," I say, mainly for Aiden's benefit. "We're neighbors. She just moved here."

"From where?" Atticus asks John in a lowered voice. "Transylvania?"

Sutton looks at him, her eyes narrowing slightly.

Atticus takes a half step back.

"She's from DC," I say. "Washington, DC."

"Cool," Kurt says. "I have a cousin who lives there."

"Are you guys ready?" Mrs. Richardson calls through the lowered passenger window. "The food's here!"

"Gotta go," Kurt says. "Unless you guys want to

come swimming with us?"

For the first time, I realize the four of them are wearing swimming trunks instead of shorts. There's a lot of neon involved.

Aiden and I look at each other.

I wait for him to second Kurt's invitation.

He stays silent.

For the first time in a long time, I'm not sure what he's thinking.

"We're waiting for someone," Sutton tells Kurt. "But thanks."

"All right. Well, catch you later," Kurt says. Behind his shoulder, I can see Atticus smirking at Sutton. From a safe distance, that is.

Aiden gives me a little wave. "Talk to you later, dude."

"Talk to you later," I echo.

As the four of them head back to Kurt's car, I push my milk shake away.

For some reason, I'm not so hungry anymore.

CHAPTER 16

AIDEN DOESN'T ANSWER his phone.

I try calling him at three o'clock.

And then at four.

And at five.

It's almost seven before he finally picks up.

Seven.

"Hey."

I almost drop the phone, I'm so surprised to actually hear his voice.

Well, no. That's an exaggeration. The phone remains firmly in my grasp. But I'm trying to make a point.

"Hey." I clear my throat. "You answered."

"Yeah, sorry."

I wait for the excuse. That he just got home. That he didn't bring his cell with him to the pool. That he did, but it was dead.

Not that I would have believed him. Just because I don't *have* a cell phone doesn't mean I don't understand how they work. I've seen enough TV to know when someone is dodging a call.

Only Aiden doesn't make an excuse. "So what's up?" he asks instead.

Other than the fact I've been calling him all afternoon? "Not much."

There's a beat of silence.

"I didn't know you were hanging out with those guys today," I blurt out. "Why didn't you tell me?"

"Kurt called after I got home. Why didn't you tell me you were going to be hanging out with your neighbor?" Aiden counters.

"I didn't know I was going to," I say quickly. "Sutton called right after you left. I was going to tell you about her," I add. "She has these pigeons, and I've been helping out with them. Some. In the mornings."

"So what? She's some sort of goth FFA chick?"

FFA stands for the Future Farmers of America. A bunch of kids from school are involved in it, mostly the ones whose parents farm for a living. They raise rabbits, or calves, or things like that, and show them at the county fair. It's kind of a big thing around here.

"She's not goth," I say automatically, even though I'm not technically sure that's true. Now that I think about it, Sutton *does* wear a lot of black. But then again, so does Neil deGrasse Tyson, and he's *definitely* not goth. An awesome scientist? Yes. Goth? No.

I'm getting off track.

"It's not an FFA thing," I explain. "She and her dad are doing it together. Like a hobby. It's more popular than you'd think. Mike Tyson raises pigeons."

"The boxer? The one who bit that guy's ear off?"

"I think they reattached it," I say. "Anyway, Sutton's cool. You'll like her."

"Yeah, okay. Listen, I should go. I've got to shower."

"Wait," I say, before he can hang up on me. I nervously switch the phone to my other ear. "Is everything okay?" The words come out in a rush, all smushed together.

"Yeah, of course," Aiden replies. His words sound smushed, too. "Why wouldn't it be?"

"I don't know. I guess I just . . . It's weird, seeing you with Kurt and those guys."

"I told you we've been hanging out," Aiden says. "You *knew* we were. It's not a big thing, okay?"

"Okay," I agree.

Aiden's right.

I know he's right.

It's not a big thing.

"It's just . . ." I can feel another blurt coming on. "You didn't invite me to go swimming with you."

There's another beat. "You were hanging out with Sutton," Aiden says. "Besides, you hate swimming."

He has a point about the swimming. I do hate it.

But is that really the reason he didn't ask me?

"So that's it? Because I ask you to do things you don't like all the time," I point out. "I still think you should join Arduino team when school starts, by the way."

I can hear Aiden snorting on the other end of the line. It's a reassuring sound, somehow.

"Yeah, right. Look, everything's cool, okay? You'll see. You're still coming to Kurt's party, right?"

Kurt's party. I'd almost forgotten about it.

"Yeah. Okay. You're right."

"I'm always right," Aiden says. "It's my curse. Listen, I'll talk to you later, okay?"

"Okay. Bye."

I hang up the phone, relieved. I feel like a giant weight has been lifted off my shoulders. Well, a moderate-size weight, at least; my shoulders aren't really built to withstand too much weight.

Checking my clock, I head downstairs and pull on my sneakers. "I'm just heading over to Sutton's," I call through to the living room, where Mom and Dad are watching a cooking show. "I'll be back soon."

"Eight thirty at the latest," Mom calls from the couch.

I nod, even though she can't see me, and head across the field. Sutton is waiting impatiently for me on her front steps, a stack of papers on her lap.

"Where have you been?" she asks, standing up.

"Sorry. Aiden called," I say, following her inside. Her house smells oniony, but in a good way. "Soup?" I ask, sniffing the air.

"Shepherd's pie. You want some?"

I wish I hadn't eaten that entire box of Cheez-Its in my room while I waited for Aiden to call me back. "I'm good," I tell Sutton, who leads the way into the living room.

"Okay," she says in a businesslike voice, spreading the papers across the coffee table. "So the Regional Director already knows that we're flying, but we need to submit the official paperwork, just to make it, you know . . ."

"Official?"

She gives me a quick grin. "Right. Mom gave me money for the entrance fee, and Dad already signed at the hospital, so we just need to fill in the rest of the stuff."

I glance down at the paper. The name "Luke Davies" is printed shakily at the bottom, next to a scrawled signature. Sutton catches me looking.

"He'd just had another dose of medicine," she says quickly. "That's not how his handwriting usually looks."

"Oh. I mean, yeah. Of course." I don't know what else to say.

"Anyway," Sutton says, clearing her throat. "I'm just going to list all of the kit's band numbers, so we don't actually have to decide who we're flying now."

I nod. The band numbers are written on these little aluminum bracelet-type thingies that the pigeons wear around one of their legs. You can personalize your bands with different colors, or your name, or something, but ours are plain. Most people band their birds when they're about a week old, so Sutton's kit had already had it done by the time she got them.

Frankly, I'm a little bit glad we didn't have to band the kit ourselves; I'm not *entirely* comfortable around pigeon feet yet.

Sutton works in silence for a few minutes, listing numbers down on the sheet. I recognize NBRC925-40 as Crow's number, but the rest are a mystery to me.

She gives a little sigh as she finishes surveying the list. "We're never going to make any real progress with only fifteen birds. Most of the other competitors probably have at least three practice kits."

Sutton's right. If we had more pigeons to work with, we could rotate them in and out of different kits, narrowing down the best birds to fly together and weeding out the ones who didn't roll.

"Next year," I say firmly, already starting to mentally plan ahead. We might need a bigger coop, but maybe I can talk to Dad, and he can . . . and then, all of a sudden, it hits me. Sutton's dad will be back next year. What if she doesn't need my help anymore? What if she doesn't *want* my help anymore? "I mean . . . or I *didn't* mean . . ." I fumble. "I'm just saying, *you* can—"

"Definitely next year." Sutton grins, cutting me off. "We'll be unstoppable."

I grin back at her, feeling ridiculously happy.

"You know what?" I ask, standing up. "I think I'll have some shepherd's pie, after all."

CHAPTER 17

I'M STILL IN a good mood when I wake up the next morning; in fact, I'm in such a good mood that my sneakers are laced before Dad even knocks on my door.

No more excuses. There's only a few weeks before school starts; it's time to get serious.

I told Dad I was going out for cross-country this fall. I told Aiden I was going out for cross-country this fall. I told *everyone* I was going out for cross-country this fall.

I *am* going out for cross-country this fall.

Even if it kills me.

I'm just turning onto the driveway when I hear someone calling my name. "Ren!" Dad shouts, pushing open the screen door. "Wait up!"

My heart sinks a little as I see he's dressed in full-on running gear, including the weird, bright red short shorts he's had forever. They're literally from before I was born.

"I almost missed you," he says, jogging toward me. "You must have been chomping at the bit this morning, huh?"

"Chomping at the bit?" I repeat.

"Like a horse?" He motions toward his mouth. "When they have a bridle on? The bit's the part that goes in their mouth."

"How old are you, exactly?" I ask. "You didn't take a buggy to school, did you?"

Dad laughs. He sets up off the driveway at a slightly faster pace than I'd like.

"Your great-grandfather used to hitch up his team to a horse-drawn sled sometimes. I remember my dad telling me stories when I was little."

My breathing is already ragged, but Dad's voice sounds perfectly normal.

"So, anyway, what's new with you?" he asks. "Mom says you've been hanging out with Sutton quite a bit lately."

I recognize his tone. It's the one he uses when he's trying to sound casual. I call it his "Cool Dad" voice.

It's slightly better than Mom's "Cool Mom" voice, but just barely.

"Yeah. Well, it's not like I have a lot of other kids to hang out with, out here," I say, trying not to pant.

Dad shoots me a look, which I pretend not to see.

"It can't be easy, being the new kid in town," he continues. "Especially when your dad is in the hospital. I'm proud of you for making friends with her, kiddo."

Part of me wants to tell him that it's not easy being the new kid *out* of town, either. But I don't trust myself to speak.

It's only partially because I'm starting to feel like I'm going to puke.

"Keep your arms down," Dad advises me, demonstrating. "When you get tired, your hands start to drift up. It costs energy. And make sure you're pushing off with your toes."

Gritting my teeth, I keep pace with him. We make it all the way to the marker Dad pointed out to me at the beginning of the summer before we turn around.

Four miles.

It's my longest run so far.

But as I collapse on the lawn, my legs aching, I don't feel proud, or happy, or even relieved.

I just feel tired.

"Nice work," Dad says, grinning down at me. "I'm going to pop in the shower. Don't forget to stretch, okay?"

The screen door slams as Dad makes his way inside.

As I stare up at the sky, I can see the kit pitching through the air.

Sutton must be wondering where I am.

I wonder if she let Squirrel and Crow fly without me.

I'm not too worried about Crow, but Squirrel is a different story. I hate to say it, but he's not exactly the sharpest pigeon in the drawer. Who knows if he'll understand when it's time to come down? Plus, he's used to me whistling when it's time for the kit to come in. Keeping things constant is the whole point of Pavlovian conditioning.

It's still early; there should be plenty of time for me to get there before they come down. But when I stand up, a sudden cramp in my calf doubles me over in pain. I bend to massage the muscle, wincing.

It's probably dehydration. I should stop by the house quick and get a drink of water. Mom and Dad are all thrilled about having our own well, now that we've moved to the country, but personally, I think it tastes horrible.

I'm poking around in the back of the fridge, looking for an abandoned bottle of water, when the sound of Dad's voice almost makes me bang my head against the shelf. "Don't forget to mark your miles. You did good this morning."

I pull back. "Right." Shutting the fridge door, I reach

for a pen. I look at the straight line that stretches across the graph for the past week. The line I've drawn while I've been hanging out with Sutton, instead of running.

I don't deserve that line.

That line is a lie.

I'll make it up, I vow, marking off today's pale blue box. Like the quote says, *today is the first day of the rest of my life.*

For a second, the thought of running every day for the rest of my life makes me want to vomit, but I push the feeling out of my head. Lance Armstrong probably felt the same way about riding a bike, and look how that turned out. He became one of the most successful athletes of all time.

Well, before everyone found out he was cheating and he had all of his medals taken away from him, anyway.

"Why haven't you left yet?" I ask Dad, capping the pen. "What about the strip mall?"

Dad grins. "I wanted to surprise you. I took the morning off. I thought we could run into Rochester. Hit up the comic store? Maybe grab some breakfast?"

My stomach rumbles at the mention of breakfast.

"Three Men doesn't open until nine," I say.

"So we'll get breakfast first." Dad leans against the counter. "What's that place you like? Stella's?"

Stella's is this retro diner that's packed with weird,

old-fashioned toy displays, and working robots, and papier-mâché superheroes that zoom across the ceiling attached to wires.

I used to love it.

When I was seven.

"I'm supposed to be meeting Sutton," I say, opening the fridge again. "Remember? I'm helping her get ready for the National Championship Fly?"

A little wrinkle appears between his eyes. "The National Championship Fly?"

"Pigeons," I remind him. "I told you she raises pigeons, right? We talked about it at dinner?"

"Pigeons!" Dad slaps his knee. "Yes! You've been helping her in the afternoons. I remember now. Sorry, things have been hectic at work. My mind is going. Bellingham Rollers, right?"

I don't bother correcting him. "Right."

"Well, why don't you call Sutton?" Dad asks. "Bring her along. The more the merrier."

"Sorry." I feel a little bad, despite myself. This is typical Dad; I barely see him for weeks, and then he'll make some sort of grand gesture like this, and expect me to be thrilled.

"I didn't know you wanted to go to Rochester," I say pointedly. "You didn't tell me." In the very back, behind some expired yogurt, I find a single bottle of

Evian. Hopefully it hasn't been here since Grandma's time.

Dad breathes in, his nose whistling a little. "You're right. Next time I'll let you know." The smile comes back, even bigger this time. "I had fun running with you this morning. Guess I'll see you tonight, okay?"

I nod. "See you tonight."

I head for the door, trying not to limp. As it swings shut behind me, I catch a final glimpse of Dad.

He isn't smiling.

CHAPTER 18

BY THE TIME I reach the tree line, the pain in my calf has almost subsided.

I thwock the empty water bottle against my thigh as I walk, marking a beat no one else can hear. It's soothing.

Step.

Thwock.

Step.

Thwock.

Sutton is standing outside the coop, staring up at the circling kit. Her shoulders are tense, like she's worried about something.

"What's going on?" I call, hurrying over to stand

next to her. "Is something wrong?"

"I let Crow and Squirrel out with the rest of the kit," she says, still looking up. "I'm worried they're not going to come back in."

I tilt my head back, scanning for them. Sure enough, two birds are off on their own, circling higher than the others.

"You let them out without me?"

"Yeah, well, you weren't here," Sutton says offhandedly.

"Sorry." I keep my eyes trained on Crow and Squirrel. "I went running with my dad. And then he wanted to take me out to breakfast in Rochester." I roll my eyes.

"Wow. Sounds awful," Sutton says flatly.

I feel a stab of guilt. Sutton would probably love to have breakfast with her dad somewhere other than a hospital room.

I shift my feet, wincing a little at the residual pain in my calf.

Beneath her baseball cap, Sutton watches me. "Did you hurt yourself?" she asks.

"It's just a cramp," I say self-consciously. "I'm dehydrated. Or it could be muscle fatigue. I just need to get back on my running schedule."

"If you say so." Sutton shrugs.

If you say so? "What does that mean?" I ask.

"I don't know. I guess I don't really get why you're going out for cross-country in the first place. Especially since you don't even like running."

"I never said that," I quickly point out. Aloud, anyway.

"Sorry," she says, not looking sorry at all. "I mean, I get that your dad used to be some big runner, or whatever, but it just kind of seems like you're trying to be someone you're not. No offense."

No offense?

How am I *not* supposed to take offense at that?

"I'm a Hall," I say as confidently as I can. "Trust me, this is who I am." I think of the box of trophies down in the basement. "There's probably Gatorade pumping through my veins instead of blood."

Sutton shrugs again. "Let's just drop it, okay?"

I open my mouth to protest, then shut it again. "Okay," I say.

We both stare up at the birds for a second. "Oh, here, before I forget," Sutton says, obviously trying to change the subject. She grabs something from just inside the coop. The issue of *Bananaman* that I lent her.

I'm relieved to see it's still in pristine condition.

"I really like it," she says, handing it back to me.

"Thanks for letting me borrow it."

"No problem. You can borrow some more, if you want." Now that I know she's going to take care of them, anyway.

Sutton smiles. A real one this time.

"You named him Crow. After Bananaman's side-kick."

"Oh. Right." I look down at the cover, embarrassed. "I just thought, you know, since they're both black. Well, blackish," I add, since our Crow is technically blue. Sutton tried to explain the different color modifiers to me the other day, when we were waiting for the kit to come down, but she didn't really know much beyond the basics.

Obviously, I did some research of my own. It turns out that male pigeons, or cocks, carry two colors, while female pigeons, or hens, only carry one. The cocks get one color from their father and one from their mother, while the hens only get one total.

So if both the father and the mother are the same color, all of the babies will be the same color, too. But if the father is blue and the mother is red, all of the boy babies will be red with flecks of blue, because red is the dominant color, but all of the girl babies will be blue, because they'll get their coloring from their father.

It's kind of fascinating, actually. Especially when you add in all the different genes that can modify the colors, like spread, dilute, recessive, and patterns.

Trying to figure it all out is like trying to solve one of the really complicated word problems from the standardized tests they're always making us take at school.

I secretly love those tests.

"Look, they're starting to come in," Sutton says, pointing up toward the kit. Grabbing the can of pigeon feed from the ground next to the coop, she scatters a little across the landing platform.

As she heads into the coop to put the can away, I start to coax the pigeons in with a low whistle. I catch sight of Crow, his wings black against the early-morning sky.

He and Squirrel are still flying a little higher than the others.

I can't believe I didn't get a chance to see how they rolled this morning. Or even *if* they rolled.

Their very first flight, and I missed it. What if they'd gotten confused and just flown away? What if something had happened to them?

Bananaman would never have left Crow to fend for himself.

I keep whistling the same low, steady note as the birds begin to maneuver onto the platform. One by one, they push their way through the door, back into the safety of the coop.

Good boy, I think, watching Squirrel drop awkwardly to the jutting piece of plywood. *Come on, Crow. Come on.* He hovers anxiously above the platform as Squirrel pokes his head inside. He's the only one left. It's his turn.

If I wasn't whistling, I'd be holding my breath.

It's touch and go for a minute, but finally, after what feels like forever, Crow drops to the platform. From where she's been watching at the door of the coop, Sutton steps cautiously over to the platform, shooing him inside.

Yes!

"All right." Sutton grins. "Way to go, Pavlov!"

I feel a rush of victory. The training actually worked! I have to actively restrain myself from pumping my fist in the air.

But as Sutton pulls the door into place, carefully fastening the latch, a tiny, creeping feeling of doubt makes its way up my spine.

I ran four miles this morning, without stopping once. Me. Lauren Hall. *Four miles. Without stopping once.*

And when I was done, I didn't feel like this: I didn't feel giddy, and excited, and *alive.*

I felt nothing.

I swallow, my throat feeling dry.

For the first time, I start to wonder if maybe Sutton's right.

Maybe I do hate running. Maybe I *am* trying to be someone I'm not.

Maybe I'm not a Hall, after all.

CHAPTER 19

A YEAR OR so before she died, Grandma's glaucoma got really bad, and she developed this thing called "tunnel vision." Basically, she lost almost all of her peripheral vision, and she could only see this little circle of things that were right in front of her. Like everything she was looking at was on the other side of this long, dark tunnel (hence the name, I guess).

Anyway, as the next couple of weeks slide by, I start to develop my own case of tunnel vision.

The National Championship Fly is the only thing I can focus on. It's the only thing I *want* to focus on.

Everything else, Dad, running, Kurt's looming back-to-school party, I shove it all over into my peripheral vision. And it all just kind of . . . fades to black.

It's probably not the healthiest coping mechanism, but what are you going to do?

"What do you want to do?" Sutton asks. "I say tomorrow is the last day we fly them before Saturday. What do you think?"

I peer inside the coop, where the kit is busy chowing down on all the dried peas they can stuff their faces with. After today, they'll go on half rations. The National Championship Fly is only five days away, and we don't want them fat and sluggish.

We've only been flying them every other day, so they'll have plenty of energy for the big day. Marathon runners do the same thing, apparently; it's called "tapering off."

"Sounds good to me," I agree. "What does your dad think?"

Sutton shakes her head. "I don't know. He's been so busy with rehab, I've barely talked to him." She nervously chips some of the polish off her thumbnail.

Shutting the door to the coop, I drop the latch in place. "We're definitely flying Squirrel and Crow, right? They've been doing awesome lately." A little too awesome, actually; the other day, Squirrel rolled so low he almost hit the ground. It was a bit of a tense moment, if I'm being honest. It reminded me of the first time I saw Sutton's pigeons, before I knew they were *supposed* to roll.

Sutton makes a final notation in the log entry she's filling out. Every time we fly the kit, we mark the date and the time, record the weather (if it's sunny, cloudy, foggy, etc., plus the wind speed and direction), and take notes on how the birds flew (how long they rolled, if they flew too low, or anything like that).

We've been taking notes on the individual pigeons, too, trying to narrow down the kit from fifteen birds to eleven before the competition. It's a little tricky trying to keep track of which bird is which from down on the ground, which is where the bingo daubers come in. Similar-looking birds with white tail feathers and wings have been marked with different colored daubers, so that when they're flying, we know which one is which. When it comes to the darker birds, we've been using binoculars; apparently you can clip some of the wing feathers to help keep track of them from the ground, but both Sutton and I are too nervous to try.

"Yeah. I mean, don't you think? Their numbers are way up," Sutton says.

I can't help the little swell of pride that pushes its way up my throat. This must be what it feels like to be a parent.

Only, you know, a little weirder.

Capping her pen, Sutton shoves it through the little hole at the top of the clipboard. "So what are you up to tonight? Want to come over? We could start season two."

In our off time, Sutton and I have been working our way through the box set of the original *Batman* TV show, with Adam West and Burt Ward. My parents gave them to me for Christmas last year. I tried to watch them with Aiden, but they weren't really his thing. He claimed the violence wasn't realistic enough.

Which is true, but not really the point, you know?

"Oh. Um . . ."

Speaking of Aiden, he's supposed to stay over tonight. His parents have a date. When Mom mentioned it over dinner last night, she wiggled her eyebrows suggestively during the word "date."

In protest, I left the table without even finishing my ice cream.

Sutton and I have been so busy with the kit that Aiden and I haven't seen each other since that afternoon at Mickey's. He hasn't even been over to help with the basement; last Tuesday he was sick, and this week he had his back-to-school doctor's checkup. Everything's seemed okay when we've talked on the phone, though. I mean, I'm not worried, or anything. It's like Aiden said; the fact that he's hanging out with Kurt isn't a big deal.

Still, it's strange. Two weeks is the longest I've ever gone without seeing Aiden. Even that one time in third grade, when he went to go visit his grandmother in Arizona, he was only gone for ten days.

"Aiden's spending the night," I tell Sutton.

"Oh." Sutton's expression doesn't change, but there's something about the way it stays exactly the same that makes me feel guilty. Like she's *trying* to not look disappointed. "Okay. No biggie."

"Sorry," I say. "His parents are staying in Rochester for the night. For a date."

Sutton wrinkles her nose. "Gross."

I nod in agreement, thinking. Maybe having Sutton there would be good. Just in case there's any lingering awkwardness between Aiden and me. She could be a buffer. Like the electrical tape I used as insulation on my portable Van de Graaff experiment, to make sure there weren't any sparks.

Plus, you know, it might be fun.

"Why don't you come over for a while, too?" I ask. "We'll just be hanging out and watching TV and stuff, but, you know . . ." I trail off, realizing I don't really have any other selling points. "You should come."

"Are you sure?" Sutton asks, looking dubious. "Aiden won't mind me crashing? I kind of got a weird vibe from him, at the drive-in."

"Don't worry," I tell her. "It won't be weird. Promise."

Sutton still doesn't look convinced.

"Come on," I wheedle.

"Okay, okay." Sutton gives me a little grin. "I'm in. Thanks."

"Cool," I say.

My oldest friend and my newest friend, together for the first time.

This'll be great.

CHAPTER 20

YOU CAN TELL Mr. and Mrs. Sorenson are going on a date because even though she's still in a pantsuit, Mrs. S's hair is loose. Usually, she wears it piled on top of her head in something Mom calls a "chignon" and Dad calls a "bun." Whatever its name is, it's very professional-looking.

Aiden slides easily out of the SUV, his high-tops kicking up little clouds of dust on the driveway. Unlike me, he doesn't need to hop, since his legs actually reach the ground.

There's a minute or two of *tell your parents thank you* and *don't stay up too late* and *you remembered clean underwear, right?* and then Aiden's parents are creeping out

of the driveway, on their way to Rochester for, er . . .
eyebrow wiggling, I guess.

Aiden slings his backpack over his shoulder. "Hey."

"Hey."

We're both quiet for a second.

Nope. Nothing weird here.

Aiden slaps away a mosquito. Despite the heat, he's
wearing jeans. Skinny jeans. They look new.

"Hey," I say, then realize I'm repeating myself. I
reach up to smooth down my hair, like it suddenly mat-
ters that it's sticking up all over the place. "So I hope
it's cool, but I invited Sutton to hang out for a while
tonight."

Aiden looks surprised. "Really? So you guys have
been, like, *hanging out*, hanging out?"

"Um, kind of."

He looks impressed. "Nice work, dude."

I can feel myself blushing, which is ridiculous. "Not
like that," I say quickly. "We're just friends." A cloud
of dust is drifting toward our house, following Sutton's
car. "Here she is," I say as Eva's station wagon turns
into our driveway. "Be cool, okay?"

"I'm always co . . ."

Aiden trails off as Eva pulls up in front of us, lowering her window. With her blonde hair hanging loose
around her shoulders, she looks like an actress. If this

was a horror movie, she'd *definitely* be killed first.

I can see Aiden's Adam's apple bobbing up and down as he swallows.

Wait. Since when does Aiden have an Adam's apple?

"Lauren, hi. Thanks so much for having Sutton," Eva says, smiling up at me. "And you must be Lauren's friend," she says, turning toward Aiden. "Nice to meet you. I'm Eva Davies."

Aiden flushes bright red. Like, really, really red. "Uh . . . hi," he mumbles.

"This is Aiden," I say helpfully.

On the other side of the car, Sutton is opening her door. As she stands up, her unnaturally red hair catches the light.

"Hey," Sutton says, looking a little wary.

Aiden nods, still tongue-tied.

"Okay, well, you kids have fun. I'll say hi to Dad for you, honey." With a final wave, Eva reverses back down the driveway. The three of us are left on our own.

Aiden finally manages to pull himself together. "Um, hey. How's it going?"

Sutton smiles cautiously at him from across the gravel.

And, just like that, I start to worry this isn't such a good idea, after all.

Maybe I didn't think this through enough. Friendly-ish greeting aside, what if Sutton and Aiden hate each other? Or worse, what if they *don't*?

What if Sutton realizes she likes Aiden better than me? What if I seem like a nerd in comparison? A short nerd who doesn't even have bangs?

What if I seem like a massive dork to Aiden, now that he has Sutton to compare me against? What if he decides he's outgrown me? In every sense of the word?

Or what if they *both* decide I'm too dorky to hang out with? When school starts, I'll have no one. I'll have to hide in a bathroom stall to eat my lunch.

A bathroom stall. I mean, can you imagine the sort of germs lurking in there? I'd give it a week, tops, before I came down with some phobia like paruresis (otherwise known as shy bladder syndrome).

Aiden breaks the silence. "I like your shirt."

Sutton looks down at her T-shirt, which reads "Jane's Addiction" in curly script. "Thanks. It's my dad's."

I force myself to relax. I'm overreacting. Obviously.

I mean, I could always eat my lunch in the science lab.

"So should we go inside?" I ask. "Mom let Dad go to the store and he bought, like, six bags of chips."

Sutton shrugs. "I could eat some chips," she says,

heading for the porch. She gives me a small smile as she passes. I smile uncertainly back.

Please let this not be a mistake.

Two hours later, I can't even remember what I was so worried about. Things are going great. We've eaten our weight in chips, and watched YouTube videos, and played video games. Sutton and Aiden are getting along just the right amount; friendly, but not *too* friendly. It's perfect.

It feels good to be hanging out with Aiden again. Even with Sutton here, it feels normal. Like how it's always been.

Even if he is checking his phone more than he used to.

Anyway, it turns out Sutton is a natural when it comes to *Beanotown Racing.* I think even Aiden's impressed with how violent she is.

"Oh, come on!" Sutton shouts, throwing herself back in her chair as her Minnie the Minx character coasts to a stop. "I thought I had him," she complains.

"You want to play again?" I ask. "Minnie kind of sucks. I'm telling you, it's all about the Bananaman racer."

Beanotown Racing is a lot like Mario Kart, only with

classic British comic book characters, like Korky the Cat, and Roger the Dodger. It's pretty much the best game ever. It came out, like, fifteen years ago, and you can only play it on the computer. Which makes it more authentic, in my opinion.

Sutton shakes her head. "My mom's going to be here soon. Besides, I'm starting to cramp up." She massages her hand, wiggling her fingers back and forth to get the blood flowing again.

I lean back against the couch cushions, which are all squashy because they're so old. When Aiden and I were little, we used to build pillow forts with the same cushions, and have these epic battles with our Star Wars action figures. It was great.

I still have all of them, packed away in a box up in my room. I wonder what Aiden would say if I brought them out right now.

I probably shouldn't risk it while there's a girl here. Even if it's just Sutton.

"Your turn," I tell Aiden, starting to hand him the laptop.

He shakes his head. "I'm good. You always beat me, anyway."

True. I shut the computer, setting it aside. Aiden takes a long swig of his soda. "So you raise birds?" he asks Sutton, shoving his phone back into his pocket. "Like, pigeons?"

"Yeah," Sutton says. "It's weird, I know."

"My dad collects stamps," Aiden says. "So it's not that weird."

"So are you into comic books, too?" Sutton asks. "Ren's been letting me borrow some of his."

I open my mouth to answer for Aiden, but he beats me to the punch.

"Yeah. I mean, I guess."

I guess?

"You love comics," I argue.

"I don't *love* comics," Aiden says. "I mean, I *like* them. But I like other stuff, too. I'm going out for basketball," he tells Sutton.

I stare at him for a second. "I didn't know you'd decided. About basketball."

"Yeah. Well, I have."

Sutton looks between the two of us.

"It's not that big of a deal." Aiden shrugs.

Yes, it is, I want to shout. *It's a huge deal. Why can't you see that?*

But instead, I just shrug, too. "Fine."

"Fine," Aiden repeats.

"Oh, look at the time," Sutton says out of nowhere,

glancing down at her watch. "My mom'll be here any second." She stands up, brushing crumbs from her lap. "But do you guys want to watch that video of the monkey riding the horse one more time before I leave?"

CHAPTER 21

"SUTTON SEEMS COOL. Kind of weird, but cool."

Aiden's voice is coming from the floor. We've shifted all my unpacked boxes to one side, leaving just enough room for him to unroll his sleeping bag and stretch out.

It's past midnight, and I should be tired.

I'm not.

"Her hair reminds me of Jean Grey," Aiden's disembodied voice says.

The Phoenix. *X-Men.* I know I should leave it alone, but I can't. "I thought you weren't that into comic books anymore."

Aiden sighs, like *I'm* the one who's being irrational.

"I never stopped liking comic books, okay? Anyway,

I think she likes you, dude."

"We're just friends. I'm helping her with her pigeons."

Why does everyone suddenly have to try to make things more than they are?

"Well, you should see if she wants to come to Kurt's party," Aiden continues. "I'm sure it'd be cool with him. What kind of swimsuits do you think goth chicks wear, anyway?" he asks.

"I told you, she's not *goth*. She's just . . . different." I shift around a little bit, searching for a comfortable position. "Anyway, I don't see what the big deal is about this party. Kurt doesn't even have a real *pool*."

In the dark, I can see Aiden sitting up. "Dude, why are you so obsessed with Kurt's pool? It's getting weird."

"I'm not obsessed. If I was going to get obsessed with something, believe me, it wouldn't be Kurt Richardson's aboveground pool."

"So, what then? Why are you mad at me?"

"I'm not mad," I insist. It's true. I'm *not* mad. I don't know what I am, exactly. I feel like someone cracked an egg at the back of my neck, and the yolk is slowly oozing down my spine.

It's not a good feeling.

"It's just . . . I don't get you," I say. "I thought everything was back to normal. But it's not. You're different. I mean, you even *look* different."

"So I bought a couple of new shirts. So what?"

"It's not about your clothes," I say in frustration. "It's about *you*. Ever since you started hanging out with Kurt, you're *different*."

"What, are you jealous?"

Of course I am. "No," I say aloud. "But it's not fair. Did you know they don't even deliver pizza this far out? I'm stuck out here in the middle of nowhere, and you're off in town, making all these new friends. Without me."

Aiden gives his pillow a thwock, flattening out the middle part for his head. "Yeah, well, I kind of didn't have a choice, dude. You moved. What did you want me to do? Sit in my basement all summer, alone? Staring at a picture of you, or something?"

Yes.

Well, no.

Not when he puts it like that. At least not the picture part.

"Besides," Aiden continues. "Even when you *were* in town, all you ever wanted to do was go to Three Men or play that boring video game."

"It's not boring. *Beanotown* is totally awesome."

"Yeah, maybe in the nineties. I mean, *Call of Duty*, dude. Ever heard of it?"

"So, what?" I try to process what Aiden's saying.

"Two months of hanging out with Kurt Richardson, and now you're too cool for everything we used to do?"

"I'm not saying that," Aiden argues. "I'm just saying sometimes I want to do some other stuff, too. Like, I love burgers, but I'm not going to eat them for every meal, you know? Sometimes I want a steak."

"You realize burgers and steak are both from the same animal," I point out.

Monophagia, I think. The practice of eating only one kind of food.

"See?" Aiden gives his pillow another punch. Harder, this time. "That's another thing. Why do you always have to do that? We get it, okay? You're smarter than everyone else. Atticus was right; you're the King of the Geeks." He sort of whispers this last part.

I feel like I'm about to throw up. "Wait, what did you say?"

"I said you're smarter than everyone, okay? We get it."

"No, not that," I say shakily. "The other part."

King of the Geeks.

Bile floods the back of my throat.

Math class, last spring.

The sign taped to my back.

I can still hear the whispers in the hallway as I walked to my locker. Feel myself grow numb as I looked over my shoulder. As I realized why everyone was laughing at me.

King of the Geeks.

I'd peeled the sign off and stuffed it in my locker. Crumpled it up like it didn't matter. Like it didn't even exist. Like the whole thing had never even happened.

Later, Aiden swore he didn't know who did it.

I'd believed him, even though he'd been walking right next to me. We never talked about it again.

"It was Atticus," I repeat. Like saying it aloud will somehow make it more believable. "Atticus made the sign. And you knew it. You *saw* him do it."

There's silence from the floor. I'm not even sure if Aiden's breathing.

"It was just a joke," Aiden finally says. His voice is so low I can barely hear him. "Okay? I'm sorry I didn't tell you. He felt really bad about it afterward."

"Oh, well then, great. As long as he felt *bad* about it, then it's totally fine."

Silence again.

"You just . . . you had your hand in the air the entire class, you know?"

I remember that day. We were going over fractions.

I'm good at fractions.

"You said you didn't know who did it." The vomit-y

feeling is getting stronger now. "You *lied* to me."

"I guess I just got sick of you showing off, okay?"

"*Showing off*?" I ask, incredulously. "I was just answering the questions."

"Yeah. All of them," Aiden mumbles under his breath. He shakes his head. "Look. I'm sorry. You're right. I should have told you. Can we just . . . drop it?"

We could drop it. It isn't too late. We could go back to pretending everything is normal.

But what would be the point?

I take a shaky breath. "That day at the drive-in. When you didn't invite me to go swimming. Tell me the truth. Was it because you were embarrassed by me?"

Aiden doesn't say anything.

"What about Kurt's party? Do you even want me to come? Or did you just invite me out of pity?"

Silence.

I can't believe this is happening.

I need to get out of here.

My legs are trembling as I push myself off the bed. I grab my blanket and pillow.

"Ren, wait."

I turn to look at him. Aiden. My best friend since kindergarten.

Right now, in the dark, he looks like a stranger.

"Do you even want to be friends anymore?" I can hear my voice cracking, but for once, I don't even care.

"Of course I want to be friends," Aiden says. "I just . . . I didn't think you'd fit in with Kurt and those guys, okay? It's not a big deal, okay, so just . . . *wait* a second, okay?"

Wrenching the door open, I stumble into the hall.

Aiden doesn't follow me.

CHAPTER 22

I CAN'T EVEN look at Aiden the next morning, let alone talk to him. The feeling is apparently mutual, which leads to a very quiet breakfast.

Honey Nut Cheerios have never sounded so loud.

Luckily, Mom has an early surgery. Aiden pretends he isn't feeling well to get out of helping with the basement, and is out the door with Mom before seven o'clock.

I'm tired.

It turns out that knowing your best friend betrayed you makes it kind of hard to sleep. Also, the couch is lumpy. But mainly it was the betrayal thing keeping me awake.

I'm just considering going back to bed for a few minutes when a faint crashing noise floats through the open kitchen windows.

I sit bolt upright, my tiredness forgotten.

Cymbals.

Sutton's using the cymbals.

But that can only mean . . .

I'm halfway out the door before I even finish the thought. I race across the field, the wet dirt pulling me down, sucking at my sneakers and making me trip.

The clanging of the cymbals grows louder as I near the coop. I can hear Sutton shouting in between crashes. "Go away! Go *away!*"

And then, suddenly, there's silence.

Sutton's back is to me as I burst through the tree line. The cymbals hang limply from her hands as she stares up at the pigeons.

She isn't yelling anymore.

"Is everything okay?" I lean forward, breathing heavily. It's a good thing I didn't finish my cereal, or I might be puking right now. "Was it a hawk?"

Sutton jumps at the sound of my voice. As she turns to face me, I can see tears on her cheeks. I straighten up. I'm too late.

"It got Squirrel." Her voice is even scratchier than

usual. Like Velcro when it gets tangled and sticks to itself in a knot.

"What?" It takes a second for me to process what Sutton is saying. "What do you mean, it *got* him?"

I look up at the kit, willing Sutton to be wrong. The hawk is nowhere to be seen, but the birds still seem scared, flying back and forth together in a tight clump.

I search for the bright spots of red that mark the undersides of Squirrel's wings.

We just re-daubed them, the other morning.

Squirrel should be easy to see.

But he's nowhere.

Sutton angrily wipes away her tears with the back of her hand. "Where were you?" she demands.

My eyes feel all hot, and weird. Like they suddenly don't fit in my eye sockets anymore. "Aiden," I say. My voice sounds weird, too. "Remember? He stayed over last night."

Sutton drops the cymbals to the ground.

I swallow.

I can't believe Squirrel's gone.

"This is all my fault. I should have been here. I could have helped. I could have scared it off." The words come faster and faster. "I should have bought an air horn. I read about them, about people using them to scare hawks away, and I was going to get one, and I forgot. I should have remembered. I should have . . ."

"Yeah, well, you didn't," Sutton says. She's purposefully not looking at me.

Her words feel like a punch in the stomach.

"I . . ." My throat feels hot and thick, and my voice doesn't come out right. "I'm sorry. I'm really, really sorry."

Sutton shrugs. "Forget about it. I guess your real friends are more important."

"That's not fair," I protest. "I didn't know Squirrel was going to—that he was going to be—"

"Killed?"

I can feel myself flinching at the word. I nod, not trusting my voice.

"Well, he was," Sutton says, turning away. She looks determinedly up at the kit, which is circling lower above the coop. "Anyway, they're coming in."

I automatically purse my lips, trying to whistle, but nothing comes out.

It doesn't matter. The kit doesn't need me; one by one they flutter down, their feet scraping against the landing board as they push their way back into the coop.

Sutton clears her throat. "I forgot the log inside. We need to mark . . ." She trails off, still not looking at me. "I'll be right back."

As Sutton heads toward her house, I pull the landing board free, shutting the plywood door and making sure it latches.

Stepping inside the coop, I tap on the light. The familiar scent of dust, and poop, and something else, that *alive* smell, washes over me.

Dumping feed into the wide, shallow pan, I open the inner door and set it on the floor. The kit goes crazy for it, their necks snapping up and down as they eat. The sound of their beaks striking against the metal pan is deafening.

But somehow it isn't quite loud enough.

I check, but Sutton has already filled the water troughs. She must have done it before the hawk attack.

Stepping back into the outer room, I lean my head against the partition. It presses against my forehead as I look closer, searching for Crow in the crowd. I can feel the wire cutting into my skin, but I don't move.

"Crow," I whisper. "Are you in there?"

It's not like I'm expecting him to answer, what with him being a pigeon.

Still, it is kind of a strange coincidence he chooses that exact moment to raise his head from the watering trough. His tiny, perfectly round eyes focus right on me, like he heard me.

"Hey," I say.

Crow tilts his head to the side, staring at me.

"I'm sorry. I'm really, really sorry. About Squirrel. I should have been here."

Crow flaps his wings a few times, turning away from the water dish. His head swivels, so he's looking at me even though he's walking in the opposite direction.

"It's going to be okay," I say, trying to make myself believe it. "You'll see. You'll make a new friend. Right?" I can hear myself pleading a little. "It's all going to be okay."

Even to my ears, the words fall flat.

As I look at Crow, standing apart from the other birds, a dull sort of pain settles in my stomach.

I'm lying.

It's not going to be okay.

It's just not.

Stepping out of the coop, I carefully fasten the door behind me. Sutton isn't back yet, but I don't wait for her.

Turning toward home, I walk away.

CHAPTER 23

I DON'T GO over to Sutton's the next morning.

I tell Mom I'm not feeling well, and she doesn't push me on it. She even offers to stay home from work, which I immediately veto.

If Mom stays home, she'll be nice to me. She'll fix up a bed on the couch, and watch terrible daytime TV with me, and make chocolate pudding from a box.

I don't deserve chocolate pudding from a box.

I don't deserve *any* pudding, full stop.

It's my fault Squirrel is gone. Sutton probably hates me, and I can't blame her. I hate myself, right now.

I keep playing it over and over in my head. If only I'd remembered to bring over the air horn. If only I could have gotten there faster. I could have helped. Maybe with the two of us, we'd have been loud enough to scare the hawk away.

I stare up at the ceiling from my bed.

Maybe we could have—

The doorbell rings and I jump a little, coming back to reality.

"Ren?" Sutton's voice floats through the open window. I sit up in confusion. "I know you're in there," Sutton calls. For a second, I'm tempted to pretend I don't hear her. "Come on, open up!"

I push out of bed and walk very slowly down the stairs, trying to brace myself. Whatever Sutton's about to say, I deserve it.

Besides, it's not like she can make me feel worse than I already do.

Taking a deep breath, I pull open the front door.

On the other side of the screen door, Sutton holds up a package of Oreos.

"I brought cookies."

I stare at them. "You brought cookies?" I repeat. "But . . . aren't you mad at me? It's all my fault," I say, the words falling fast. "If I had been there, I could have helped. I could have—"

"Ren." Sutton cuts me off. "Just listen, okay? I'm sorry about yesterday. I didn't mean to blame you, or whatever. It's not your fault. It just . . . it happens."

I shake my head.

"It's not okay. Squirrel's gone. It's my fault, and now Crow is going to be all by himself."

"He's not going to be all by himself. He's got the entire kit."

"It's not the same," I insist. My voice breaks a little on the last word, making me sound about seven years old. I don't even care. "It won't be the same."

On the other side of the door, I ball up my fists as tight as I can, squeezing until my knuckles ache.

It doesn't help.

"Can I come in?" Sutton asks. "It's kind of weird, just standing here."

I let out my breath in a big whoosh. "Yeah. Sorry." Sutton opens the door, both of us wincing a little at the screech. I lead the way into the living room, and we sit down on the couch. Sutton pushes the box of Oreos in my direction.

I'm not really hungry, but it feels like a peace offering, so I rip open the package and take one.

"I should have been there," I say again, trying to twist open the cookie. My fingers are clumsy, and I smash part of it, the crumbs falling all over my lap. "If it hadn't been for Aiden, I *would* have been."

"It's not Aiden's fault, either," Sutton says. "I shouldn't

have said that yesterday. I was just . . . I don't know . . . jealous, I guess. But, I mean, I get that you have other friends. It's cool."

"*Had* other friends," I tell her. "We had a fight."

"So? My friends and I fight all the time," Sutton says. "It doesn't mean anything."

"This is different. He lied to me. He's *been* lying to me." Just thinking about it makes me feel nauseated. I set my broken Oreo on the edge of the coffee table, uneaten.

Sutton shrugs. "Everyone lies. At least sometimes."

"Not me." I even told Aiden the truth about that time I accidentally ripped a tiny corner of his *Wolverine and the X-Men #1.*

"Really?" she asks. "Because your dad showed me your running chart thingy the other night, when I ran into him in the kitchen."

Oh.

"Sorry. It just kind of . . . happened. And a lot of the chart is real," I point out. "I *was* running. Just, you know . . . not lately."

I look down at my running shorts, which I put on this morning out of habit. There's a mustard stain near the hem. It's been there for weeks now.

For *weeks.*

As I stare down at the spot, I realize Sutton is right.

I *have* been lying. But not just to Dad; I've been lying to myself, too.

"I don't think I want to go out for cross-country." The words feel heavy, leaving my mouth. Like once they're gone, I'm somehow lighter.

Sutton looks like she's trying not to roll her eyes. "Really? You think?"

"It's just . . . I told everyone I was going to do it, you know? This was supposed to be my chance to prove I was good enough. But I'm not."

"Good enough at what?" Sutton demands. "Running in a straight line without falling down? No offense, but it's not like it's some big accomplishment, or anything."

She has a point. Still. "My dad's going to be disappointed." He'll try to hide it, I know. But he won't be able to help the look in his eyes when he realizes I'm not like him, after all. That I'm not an athlete. That I'm just a geek.

The King of the Geeks.

"He'll get over it," Sutton says authoritatively. "Trust me. You don't have to prove anything to anyone."

I think about Aiden.

About how he's embarrassed by me. About how he thinks I won't fit in with his new friends. About how I don't even know him anymore.

Sutton's right. I don't *have* to prove anything to anyone.

But that doesn't mean I *can't*.

"Hey, Sutton?" She looks up at me.

"Yeah?"

I take a deep breath.

"Want to go to a party this Friday?"

CHAPTER 24

MOM PRACTICALLY SNORTS coffee out of her nose when I tell her I want to go clothes shopping.

Lowering her cup, she stares at me like I'm speaking Portuguese, or I've suddenly sprouted a third eyeball.

"You want to go where?"

"Clothes shopping. Can you take me today? After work?"

"Who's going shopping?" Dad asks, wandering into the kitchen.

"Ren wants to go," Mom tells him. "For *clothes*."

"Clothes?" Dad pretends to stagger backward in shock. "My heart," he groans, clutching at his chest. "I'm too old for shocks like these."

I roll my eyes. I can see why Sutton does it so much; it's satisfying.

"So can you take me?" I ask Mom.

"Sure," she says. Her phone begins to buzz, and she picks it up from the table. "We can go shopping. I'll even take off a little bit early, okay?"

"Thanks. Oh, and maybe we can get my hair cut, too."

She gapes at me a little, then brushes past Dad to go take the phone call. He grabs a banana from the counter. It looks small in his hands. "So how was your run, kiddo?"

My first instinct is to shrug. To tell him it was fine, and let it drop.

But instead, I force myself to meet his eyes.

I'm done lying.

"Um, is it okay if we talk for a second?"

"Sure." He sets the banana back down, looking concerned. "What's up?"

You can do this, Ren. Just rip off the Band-Aid.

"I hate running and I don't want to join the cross-country team."

Dad blinks, taken aback. "You hate running?"

Okay. I may have ripped that one off a little bit too quickly.

"I mean . . . I think maybe . . . I just think that running isn't really my . . . you know . . . thing," I finish weakly.

A line appears on Dad's forehead. "So what have we been doing all summer then? Why have I been helping you train?"

"I'm sorry. I didn't mean to waste your time, or anything. I thought I'd, you know . . . get better at it. But I didn't."

"The only way you get better at running is by running," Dad says. "You put in the work, and you get the results. That's what I did. That's what my cross-country kids did." He points at my running chart, hanging on the fridge. "It's not too late to get your totals up before school starts."

I glance over at the chart. "Right. About that."

Dad looks at me, waiting for me to go on.

I suck in a deep breath. "I haven't actually been running lately. I'm not just hanging out with Sutton in the afternoon. I've been there in the morning, too, helping her with her pigeons."

His shoulders pull back, a little.

"You've been lying to me?"

It feels just as terrible as I thought it would. I can feel my face growing hot. "Not lying, exactly," I say hastily.

"I was going to make it up. I promise. But then Sutton needed my help, and I don't know. I just . . . didn't."

Dad doesn't say anything.

"It's not like there's really a point to me going out for the team," I babble, trying to fill the silence that's threatening to swallow the kitchen whole. "It doesn't matter how much work I put in. I'm never going to be as good as you were. I mean, look at you, and look at me."

"You just haven't hit your growth spurt yet," Dad says. He's looking at me, but not quite *looking* at me, somehow.

"It doesn't matter," I say, trying to make him understand. "I could be seven feet tall, and it wouldn't matter. I'm never going to win State, or be the team captain, or have a box full of trophies in the basement. I'm just not. I'm not *you*, okay?"

"You're right."

I feel a tiny rush of hope. Maybe he understands, after all.

"You're not me," Dad continues. "In fact, right now it feels like I don't even know *who* you are. The Ren I know doesn't lie to his parents."

And, picking up his banana, he walks out of the kitchen.

I'm still staring at the door with hot, scratchy eyes when Mom bustles back in. "So, shopping today?" she asks, smiling at me as she reaches for the remains of her toast.

"Yeah," I say dully. "Sounds great."

CHAPTER 25

"WHOA."

I can see Sutton's eyes widen as she slides into the car next to me. It's Friday night, and Mom is about to drop us off at Kurt's party.

Together.

"You look . . ." She gives a little shake of her head, like she can't believe what she's seeing.

I look down at myself. I don't look *that* different, do I?

Sure, I got a haircut. It still sticks up, only this time it's on purpose, and I'm using this weird "styling product" to hold it in place. And I'm wearing a new shirt, too. A button-down. It's covered with tiny lobsters that are eating French fries. Why lobsters would eat French fries, I have no idea, since generally their diet consists mainly of fresh seafood. Sometimes they even eat other lobsters, which technically makes them cannibals.

Still, the woman at the store said it was cool, so who am I to argue?

My swim trunks are baggy and knee-length, and are covered with neon stripes. According to the same sales clerk, they're *supposed* to look like they're going to fall off any second. "Riding low," she called it. I double-knotted the string at the waist when I was putting them on, just to be safe.

I don't have any socks on inside my slip-on shoes, and my feet are all sweaty.

I'm sweaty everywhere, actually, even though Mom is blasting the air-conditioning.

"Nice shorts," Sutton says. "Very . . . bright." She's wearing cutoffs and a black tank top. I can see the straps of her swimsuit peeking out beneath.

It's a totally normal, non-gothy one.

Another thing Aiden was wrong about.

"Thanks," I tell her. "They're new."

"Hi, Sutton," Mom calls from the front. "Ren says your big competition is tomorrow. Good luck!"

"Thanks, Mrs. Hall. And thanks for the ride."

Mom smiles in the rearview mirror. "Of course."

Sutton lowers her voice, leaning in toward me. "Is there something going on that I should know about?"

"What?" I ask innocently. "I don't know what you mean."

"Uh-huh." She eyes me suspiciously, but lets it drop. I spend the rest of the ride staring out the window as she and Mom talk about school, and whether or not Sutton is going out for any activities.

To my surprise, I learn that she's thinking about signing up for gymnastics.

As we pull up in front of Kurt's house, I can feel my stomach kind of . . . churning. Maybe I shouldn't have had so much pizza for lunch.

"You okay?" Sutton asks, unbuckling. "You look a little . . . green."

"I'm fine. Just excited. I love pool parties."

"Okay." She gives a little shrug. "Let's go then."

I force myself to unsnap my seat belt. Are my hands shaking a tiny bit? Maybe I'm hypoglycemic. I make a mental note to check the symptoms online later.

"Have fun!" Mom gives us a little wave. "Call when you want me to pick you up!"

All right. This is it.

I open the door.

Kurt's family lives in one of the new subdivisions at the edge of town. Their house is big, with an attached, three-car garage and boulders scattered artfully around the yard. It's all very beige.

In every sense of the word.

I can hear music, and people laughing, and the occasional screech coming from the backyard. I hesitate. Do we ring the front doorbell? Go around back? I don't know the correct etiquette for crashing your best friend's new best friend's pool party.

Not that we're crashing. I mean, I *was* invited.

Technically, at least.

Luckily, Sutton seems to know what to do. As she heads for the side of the house, I follow. My feet slip a little in my new shoes.

Maybe socks were invented for a reason.

I'm not exactly sure what I'm expecting as we turn into the backyard, but as much as it pains me to admit, Kurt's pool is actually pretty great. It's a lot bigger than I expected, with a wooden deck surrounding it and an attached, screened-in gazebo. A volleyball net is strung down the middle of the pool, and there's even a little waterslide.

"Whoa," Sutton says. "Nice."

I shrug. "It's not that nice," I say under my breath.

I can feel Sutton giving me a look, but I ignore her.

A lot of people are already here, splashing in the pool or clustered in little groups on the deck, talking. There's music coming from somewhere, something loud and thumpy, where you can't make out the words. I recognize Atticus and John running around with Super Soakers, making a couple of the girls shriek every time they get too close.

My stomach flips at the sight of Atticus, but I force myself to act like everything's fine.

For a second, I think Aiden isn't here yet. Then I spot him, sitting at the edge of the pool next to Madison. He's talking to Kurt, who's floating around in some kind of inflatable armchair.

Madison's bikini is small.

I hope she's not planning on going in the water in it.

Aiden doesn't see me at first. But as John races past, Aiden turns his head to avoid the stream of water coming from John's squirt gun.

Our eyes meet.

There's a long sort of pause, the kind where if this was a movie, everything would slow way down, and you'd be able to hear the sound of my heart beating above the background noise. Thump. Thump. Thump.

Aiden turns away first.

"Come on." Steeling myself, I grab Sutton's hand. "Let's mingle."

CHAPTER 26

SUTTON'S PALM IS really dry compared to mine.

"What are you doing?" she asks, looking down at our locked hands.

Instead of answering, I head toward the deck, practically pulling her up the stairs behind me. I'm sure not *everyone* turns to look at us as we make our way onto the deck, but it definitely feels like it.

Most of them look confused. Aiden's expression is a little harder to read.

I raise my left hand, giving a little wave in Kurt's direction. I don't want to drop Sutton's hand until I'm sure everyone's seen me holding it. "Hey," I say. "Uh, thanks for having us. Cool pool."

I can hear my blood pumping in my ears. I feel like the "King of the Geeks" sign is still hanging from my back for everyone to read. Like when they look at me, that's all they can see.

Like they're about to start laughing at me again.

Gelotophobia, I think grimly. *The fear of being made fun of.*

If Kurt thinks it's strange that we're at his party, he doesn't show it. "Hey, man."

He slides off his armchair thingy, hauling himself out of the pool in front of us. "Thanks for coming." I mentally scan the remark for sarcasm, but it seems clear. Either he's a really good actor, or he genuinely doesn't mind that I'm here.

I feel a twitch of relief.

Tiny drops of water flick onto the wood as Kurt pushes his hair back. "What's going on?" he asks Sutton.

"Not much," she says. "I hope it's okay I'm crashing your party."

"Yeah, of course. The more the merrier." He pushes his bangs back again, smiling at Sutton.

For some reason, I feel a little twinge of jealousy.

Sutton pulls her hand free. She wipes her palm on the front of her shorts, which is a little offensive. My hands aren't *that* sweaty. "Cool."

I can see Aiden watching us from the side of the pool,

although he's trying to be all stealthy about it.

"So do you know who your teacher is for this year?" Kurt asks.

"Mrs. Thompson," Sutton says.

"Hey, Kelsey has Mrs. Thompson, too. You wanna meet her? She's right over—"

"Actually," I interrupt, "we're going to get some food first. Right, Sutton?"

She shoots me an annoyed look, but follows me into the gazebo. "You're being really weird, you know."

"Look." I point at the table. "There's a nacho cheese machine. You want some nachos?"

"No." She crosses her arms in front of her. "I want you to stop being weird."

"I'm not being weird," I protest. Loading up a plate with chips, I begin pumping liquid cheese on top of them. It looks a little disgusting, but now that I've started, I can't stop. I pile a bunch of black olives on top for good measure.

"Come on," I say, grabbing two sodas. Regular Cokes, not the fancy European kind. Kurt's mom must not want to waste those on his friends. "There's a couple of chairs open over there."

Avoiding her gaze, I walk back outside.

To my relief, she follows me.

An hour later, everything is going great.

No, better than great. You could even say *swimmingly.*

Ha. I kill myself.

Sutton and I have really made a splash.

Ha. Okay. That was the last one, I promise.

Anyway, it turns out everyone wants to meet "the new girl with the hair," as I overheard Kelsey calling Sutton. Sutton's barely had time to touch the nachos I made for her; people keep coming up and introducing themselves.

I've had my share of stares as well. According to Natalie Blum, she didn't even recognize me.

To be fair, I don't think I've ever talked to her before.

Kind of for good reason, it turns out, since all she wanted to talk about was the latest episode of some TV show neither Sutton nor I had ever seen.

Still. It was exciting. Natalie is one of the most popular girls in our grade.

We talked to Margot Abbott, too, who told me she thought my shirt was really cool, and Miles Hagedorn, and Quentin Laughlin. We even spent twenty minutes talking about basketball with Kurt and John.

I don't know much about basketball, so I spent a lot of time nodding and making "uh-huh" sorts of sounds in the back of my throat.

At the end of the conversation, Kurt and John both high-fived me.

It was . . . strange.

Now Sutton and I are sitting near the edge of the pool, watching Kurt and a bunch of people playing water volleyball. The nauseous feeling in my stomach is long gone, and I'm stuffing my face with a fresh plate of nachos.

Even the sight of Aiden standing directly in front of me, setting up the ball for Kurt, doesn't bother me. In fact, I'm glad he's here, just so he can see how well I'm fitting in with everyone.

So he can see how wrong he was about me.

Everyone shouts in excitement as Kurt spikes the ball past John's reach. It lands on the other side of the net, sending a spray of water over everything, including my nachos.

Sutton wipes her arm dry. "Hey, so how much longer do you want to stay?" she asks. "Because if we left right now, we'd still have time to watch a movie."

Is she serious?

"Are you serious?" I ask aloud. "You want to leave already?"

She shrugs. "Kind of."

"Why?" I ask in bewilderment. "This is awesome."

Sutton looks at me. "Awesome? Are you serious?

People are staring at me like I'm some kind of alien."

"That's not true. They're just . . . interested."

She nods in Atticus's direction. "That guy asked me if I had any *tattoos*. Where would I even *get* a tattoo? I'm *eleven*."

"Okay, fine. Atticus is terrible," I admit. "But he's just one guy. Everyone else seems nice, right?"

Another shrug. "I guess. I mean, are they actually your friends? Because it doesn't really seem like you guys have a lot in common. Or even you know . . . know each other. And what's going on with you and Aiden? You haven't even looked at each other this whole time."

That's not true. We've actually looked at each other a lot. Just not when we thought the other one would notice.

"And what was that whole conversation with Kurt and John? You don't even *like* basketball."

"I *could* like basketball. Maybe I've always just been prejudiced because I'm short." And because it's really boring. And I don't like the squeaking noise tennis shoes make on the floor of the court. And because I don't really understand the rules.

Okay. I probably don't like basketball.

"Let's just stay another half an hour," I say. "You haven't even been in the pool yet."

Sutton looks disinterestedly down at the water.

"Yeah. I don't know. Maybe I'm just nervous about the Fly tomorrow."

I take another huge bite, cheese dripping down my fingers. I've got to talk Mom into investing in a nacho machine. "It's going to go great."

"You think?" She looks hopeful for about a second before the wrinkles on her forehead return. "I don't know. I checked online. Some guy in Austin got, like, two hundred points earlier today. We're probably going to get crushed. Especially now that we don't have Squirrel."

I try to ignore the stab of guilt in my stomach. Logically, I know Sutton is right; it's not my fault Squirrel is dead.

But sometimes it's hard to make the rest of me believe my brain.

"It's our first year. I mean, *your* first year," I tell Sutton. "No one expects you to win. Not yet, anyway," I add. Sutton tends to be a little sensitive when it comes to people not taking her as a serious competitor.

"Maybe you're right. I just don't want to disappoint my dad." She brushes an imaginary drop of water off her knee. "Part of me thought he was actually going to be well enough to be there tomorrow. Just so he could at least *watch*, you know?"

I'm momentarily distracted as the volleyball hits the

water, raining chlorinated water all over my nachos again. "Smacked!" John howls. He does a little victory lap around the side of the pool, high-fiving the people sitting on the edge.

As he nears Sutton and me, I hold my hand out, searching for something to say. "Nice one, dude!"

Sutton completely ignores John and stares at me instead. A second later she pulls her legs out of the pool, reaching for her flip-flops. "All right. That's it. I can't watch this anymore. I'm done."

"Wait, watch what?"

"*You*. Sucking up to Kurt and his friends. It's ridiculous."

"What are you talking about?" I protest. "I'm not."

"Save it," she says, jamming her flip-flops onto her feet. "You're not fooling anyone, okay? These people aren't your friends. You're obviously trying to prove something to Aiden. Or to yourself. I don't know. And you know what? I don't care. I'm done."

She stands up. "Enjoy the rest of the party, *dude*. I'll find my own ride home." As she takes the stairs two at a time, heading into the house, I stare after her in shock.

What just happened?

CHAPTER 27

MY FIRST THOUGHT is to follow Sutton into the house.

But then what? Even if she'll talk to me, I have no idea what to say. I don't even know if I *want* to talk to her.

I mean, who does she think she is?

This party is *great*.

I'm having a *great* time.

Sutton doesn't know what she's talking about. She doesn't know *me*. She met me less than five weeks ago. I've known most of these people my *entire life*.

And sure, we've never really hung out before, but so what? Like the quote says, *there's no time like the present.*

I shift a little on the wooden deck, looking down at my soggy nachos.

Excellent. Now I've lost my appetite.

"Hey, Hall! You wanna get in on this?" Kurt hoists the volleyball in my direction, looking at me questioningly.

As much fun as showing off my nonexistent volleyball *and* swimming skills sounds, I'll pass.

I shake my head. "No, thanks."

"Come on, man. Think fast!"

Before I know what's going on, Kurt lobs the volleyball in my direction.

It's like something out of a nightmare.

Flustered, I drop the nachos on my lap, reaching out for the ball. Only I've forgotten I'm sitting on the edge of the pool. As I stretch out my arms, my center of balance tips forward. I belly flop into the water with a loud splash.

Water floods my nose, the chlorine burning the back of my throat, making me feel like I'm going to choke. The pool is five feet deep; I'm so short I have to stand on tiptoes to breathe, wiping my nose and my eyes with the back of my hand.

Nachos float around me like dead leaves.

"Dude, are you okay?"

I can hear Kurt's voice, but his body is just a blurry

lump. My glasses must be somewhere at the bottom of the pool.

I cough, trying to clear some of the water out of my lungs.

And then I hear it.

A laugh.

Someone is laughing at me.

I whip my head around, trying to pinpoint where it's coming from. But without my glasses, it's useless. I can't see anything.

Another laugh, this time somewhere behind me.

And then another.

It's the sign on my back all over again.

I want to sink to the bottom of the pool. To curl up into a ball, and close my eyes, and just . . . disappear.

What was I thinking, coming here? What did I expect?

"Nice throw, dude. My grandma has better aim."

It's Aiden's voice. Even without my glasses, I know. I recognize it.

He's making fun of Kurt.

"Yeah, man, I thought you were a ballplayer?" It's Atticus's voice, I'm pretty sure. "You throw like my grandpa."

"You *look* like my grandpa," Kurt retorts. "Hey, you okay, Hall? My bad."

"Um . . ." I cough again. "I'm fine. I just . . . I lost my glasses."

"I'll get 'em." It's Aiden again. Popping his head under the water, he disappears. "Here," he says, re-emerging a second later. He hands me my glasses.

"Thanks," I say uncertainly. I slip them on. They're covered with water drops, but at least I can see. Kind of.

Everyone's still looking at me, but they're not laughing anymore. Not like *that*, anyway.

"Hey, look," Atticus points. "Pool nachos." Snagging a passing tortilla chip, he pops it into his mouth.

"Gross, dude!"

"That's disgusting!"

Kurt laughs. "Sick, dude. Hey, Sorenson, toss me that ball, would you?"

And just like that, it's over.

A couple people grin at me as I drag myself out of the pool, but most people are too busy watching Atticus and John dive for pool nachos to pay much attention to me. I head around the side of the house, my shoes squelching with each step.

I'm hesitating outside the front door, wondering how I'm going to get to a phone without completely flooding the Richardsons' house, when I hear someone coming up behind me.

"Here."

I turn. Aiden tosses a towel in my direction.

"I thought you might need this."

"Thanks." I take the towel. Sitting down on the ground I pull my shoe off, tipping it upside down to let the water run out.

"No problem." He hesitates for a second. I empty my other shoe.

"Cool," he says at last. "Well, see you later, I guess." He turns to go.

Good.

I didn't want to talk to him, anyway.

"Wait," I hear myself saying. "Thanks. For, you know . . . helping me. Just now. In the pool."

He turns back. "Yeah. I mean, Kurt's a good guy." Sitting down next to me, he plucks a couple of blades of grass. The Richardsons' grass is really, really green. "He wouldn't have tried that on purpose."

I pull my shoes back on. "Can I ask you something?" I concentrate on my shoes, not looking at him.

"Yeah. What?"

"Did you help Atticus write the sign? The one . . . well, you know. That one?"

Aiden shakes his head. "No. But I should have told you. It was stupid. *I* was stupid."

"You're not stupid," I say automatically. "Remember

when we found my uncle's old Rubik's Cube? You did it in, like, two minutes. Plus, you know what bottle episodes are. And you can draw. Your Bananaman is better than the original."

"Yeah. Well, no offense to John Geering, but he wasn't exactly Picasso, you know?"

"I'm just saying." I shrug. "I'm not that smart, either. I'm just good at memorizing stuff. I'm like . . . a parrot, or something. 'Polly want a cracker?'"

"Shut up. You don't even like crackers."

I can't help grinning a little, even though I'm soaking wet, and I just made a fool of myself, and I'm not even sure if I have any friends anymore. "They're just so *dry*, you know? Who wants their food to be that dry?"

Xerophobia, my brain whispers. *The fear of dryness.*

Aiden pulls up some more grass, twirling it between his fingers. His hands are getting bigger, too. Pretty soon they'll be meathooks, like Dad's.

"Anyway," I say. "Sorry. I know I'm a pain, sometimes. I get why you're embarrassed to be around me. Why you want to be friends with Kurt instead."

"I'm not embarrassed," Aiden says. "And I don't want to be friends with Kurt *instead* of you. It's not, like, all or nothing, you know? Why can't I be friends with both of you?"

When he puts it like that, it sounds logical. "I don't

know," I shrug. "You're just . . . so different, you know? You're going out for basketball next year, and you'll sit with Kurt and everyone at the jock table, and I'll just be . . . the same."

Kurt's parents aren't going to be very happy when they see the bald patch of lawn Aiden's made.

Part of me is waiting for Aiden to tell me I'm wrong. That everything's fine. That it'll all go back to normal, once school starts.

But another part of me knows that's not going to happen.

I look around at Kurt's yard.

Sutton was right.

I don't belong here. I don't know why I was pretending I did.

This isn't who I am.

I'm not a sports guy. I'm not cool. I'm not popular.

I'm not like Kurt, or Atticus, or John.

I'm not like Aiden.

I'm a geek.

I'm the King of the Geeks.

And maybe that's okay.

"We'll still hang out," Aiden says. "Just not, you know . . . all the time."

I nod, not looking at him. The chlorine is burning the back of my throat again.

"Besides," Aiden says. "What about Sutton? And the pigeons, or whatever they are? I'm not the only one who's doing new stuff, right?"

"She left," I admit. "I don't even know what happened. One minute we're talking about her dad and everything is fine, and then the next minute . . ." I trail off. "Girls are complicated."

Aiden shrugs. "Yeah, but all that stuff with her dad, it's gotta suck for her, right?"

"Yeah," I admit. "I mean, I guess so."

"When's he getting out of the hospital, anyway?"

"I don't know."

"But he's going to be able to, like, walk again and stuff, right?" Aiden asks.

"I don't know," I say.

And then it hits me.

How is it possible that I have no idea what's going on with Sutton's dad? I mean, I know she said she didn't want my pity when she first told me, but I've barely even *asked* about him.

No wonder she left.

"Can I use your phone?" I ask Aiden. "I have someplace I need to be."

CHAPTER 28

I'M ABOUT TO knock on Sutton's front door when it hits me; Sutton's dad may not be here to see it, but the Fly is still tomorrow morning; I'm standing in front of the wrong door.

Turning around, I cut across the lawn and head out to the field. It's getting darker now, and I can see the light spilling out through the open door of Sutton's coop.

"Sutton?" I give a little knock to the side of the loft. "Are you in there? It's me."

As she steps into the doorway, she doesn't seem surprised to see me.

She's looked better, I can't help noticing.

Her fiery hair is scraped back into a bun, with straggly pieces escaping at the front, and her eyes are all puffy and red. She's wearing baggy plaid pajama pants and another one of her dad's T-shirts, which reads "Violent Femmes" across the front.

Something tells me Mom would *not* approve of their music.

"Hey." Her voice is dull. "What are you doing here?"

"I had my mom pick me up," I tell her.

"Oh."

Silence.

It seems like there's been a lot of awkward silences in my life lately.

"I'm sorry," I say. "You were trying to tell me about your dad, and I just . . . I'm sorry. I'm a terrible friend."

Swinging the door shut behind her, Sutton sinks down on the step. "You're not a terrible friend, Ren. I'm the one who told you not to be weird about him."

"There's a difference between being weird about something and completely ignoring it," I point out. "I can't even imagine what you're going through. I'm sorry. I shouldn't have made you do it alone."

Sutton looks at the coop. "I haven't been alone. And besides, you've been here. I probably wouldn't even be flying tomorrow, if you hadn't been helping me."

"It's not enough. I'm going to do better," I promise.

"It's not just about the pigeons. I mean, we're *friends*, right?"

She grins. "Yeah. We're friends."

It feels like a weight has just slid off my shoulders. "And sorry about before, too," I add. "The party. You were right. I don't really fit in with those guys. They're Aiden's friends, not mine."

Saying it out loud makes me realize how true it is.

And how it's okay.

"Did you at least figure things out with Aiden?" Sutton asks.

"I don't know," I say. "Maybe. I hope so." Just because things are different, doesn't mean they're bad, right?

Sutton sighs. "Big day, huh? Do you want to just watch a movie, or something? Zone out?"

There's a plan brewing in my head.

I wouldn't even call it a plan yet, actually.

But there's an *idea* for a plan in my head.

And it's a good one.

I nod. "Yeah. Let's do it."

CHAPTER 29

DAD IS WAITING up for me when I get home. He's sitting at the dining room table, a cardboard box resting on the table in front of him.

The guilt that I've managed not to think about for the past couple of days slams back into my stomach.

"Hey," I say. "Sorry, I know it's late."

"Mom says you came home early from the party?"

"Yeah." I clear my throat. "It was kind of a bust, actually."

"Ah," Dad says. "Want to talk about it?"

"Not really," I say honestly.

He nods. "So, listen. About yesterday. What you said about not wanting to join the cross-country team."

My stomach gives a little flip of dread. "I'm sorry," I say quickly. "I know I shouldn't have lied to you. I—"

He holds up his hand, cutting me off. "I'm the one who should be apologizing. I was just . . . taken aback, I guess. I thought you *liked* running."

"I *wanted* to," I say. "I mean, I tried to like it."

Dad's lips curve up a little at the edges. "I'm still not happy that you lied to me, but I'm more upset that you thought you *had* to. I've been putting too much pressure on you, kiddo."

"No," I protest. "I mean, I'm the one who asked for your help, remember?"

"I should have realized what was going on. I'm your dad. I'm supposed to know things about you." He shrugs. "It's kind of my job."

"I'm sorry," I say again. "I know you're disappointed. I thought that maybe because I'm a Hall, I'd be good at it," I admit, realizing how ridiculous it sounds. "That I'd take after you, or something. But I guess it doesn't work that way."

"Look in the box," Dad says.

"What?"

"The box," he repeats, pointing toward the table. "Look in it."

I step forward, confused, and flip the cardboard flaps open.

It's full of comics. Old ones, even older than the ones I'm into. *Popeye*, and *Little Lulu*, and *Tarzan of the Apes*. "Whoa. Where did you get these?" I ask.

"They were Grandpa's," Dad says. "I found them in the basement. I'd forgotten all about them, until you mentioned those old trophies of mine down there."

"These are awesome," I say, flipping through the box. *Smilin' Jack*? I've never even *heard* of that one. "How did I not know we had these?"

"I'm obviously overpaying you and Aiden," Dad says, grinning. But a second later, he looks serious again. "Just because I like running doesn't mean you need to. You don't need to worry about being a *Hall*, okay? You just have to worry about being yourself."

I stare down at the box full of Grandpa's old comics, inhaling the warm, dusty scent. "Okay," I say, feeling a tiny flood of happiness. I mean, who *knows* what's buried at the bottom of the box? "Are you sure?" I ask.

"Please," Dad scoffs. "Can the Silver Surfer fly?"

Actually, the Silver Surfer *can't* fly. He uses his surfboard-like craft to travel through space. But I get what Dad's going for.

I force myself to step away from the box. "Um, just so you know, it's the same for you, too."

Dad looks surprised. "For me?"

"I just meant, you know, you don't have to pretend to

like comics anymore. If you don't want to. I mean, it's nice of you to try," I say, not wanting to hurt his feelings. "But I know you're not really that into them."

Dad smiles. "I've maybe been overdoing it a little, huh?"

I hold up my thumb and index finger close together. "Maybe a little."

"Sorry. I guess I've just been feeling a little guilty lately. I know the move's been hard on you."

"I don't know," I say, thinking about Sutton and the kit. "I'm actually starting to like it out here."

"Really?" Dad asks in surprise.

"Yeah," I say. "I'm even thinking of unpacking my room."

He stands up, stretching out his arms. "Well, let's start tomorrow, kiddo. It's late."

"Yeah. Umm, about that. Before we go to bed, I kind of need . . . a favor."

In the end, we have to estimate the square footage in a couple of places, and we can't decide on cement or crushed gravel when it comes to the pathways, but on the whole, the plans turn out pretty well.

As the sun starts to rise out the window, the sky above Sutton's house turns the same shade of peach as the walls in my room.

It's nice, unless you start thinking about how all the peachy color is actually just pollution. Sometimes scientific knowledge is a curse.

"And that's basically it," I tell Dad, stifling a yawn. "Oh. Except for you get extra points the faster they roll."

"On top of the points for distance?"

"Yep."

On the laptop screen, a kit of rollers plummets in slow motion toward the ground. We've watched it a bunch of times now. "Fascinating," Dad says again, shaking his head.

"I should probably get going." I start to gather up the plans, which are strewn all over the kitchen table. We actually finished hours ago, but, by then, we'd had too much caffeine to even think about sleeping. It was kind of fun, though, staying up with Dad. Like a really weird sleepover, where one of us drank coffee instead of soda.

Dad nods absently, still staring at the screen. "You know," he says. "Your mom's been so busy, she hasn't even started planning her garden yet. That shed out back is just going begging." He looks up at me. "What do you say next year we give Sutton and her dad a run for their money?"

"Really?"

A giant yawn almost splits his face in two. "Ask me

again after I've slept," he says, grinning.

I can't help grinning back.

"Thanks again for everything, Dad. Really."

"My pleasure, kiddo. Tell Sutton good luck for me, will you?"

"Luck is preparation meeting opportunity," I inform Dad, heading for the door.

"Benjamin Franklin?"

"I heard it from Oprah," I call over my shoulder.

I'm jittery with nerves, and caffeine, and sugar as I head across the field, the drawings tucked carefully under my arm. It's a perfect day for the Fly; cloudy, with a light breeze, and just a hint of moisture in the air.

I wonder if Sutton managed to get any more sleep than I did, or if she's been awake the entire night, too.

Something tells me it's probably the second option.

As I near the house, I can see an unfamiliar truck parked in the driveway; the judge must already be here. "Sutton?" I call out toward the coop. "Are you in there?"

Her answer comes from the direction of the house. "We're in here!"

I pause to straighten my shirt before opening the door. Hopefully the judge has a sense of humor, because I'm wearing my favorite "Bananaman vs. Doctor Gloom" tee, for luck.

Don't tell Oprah.

"Sutton?" I poke my head inside the house. "Mrs. Davies?"

Sutton darts into the hallway, looking as manic as I feel. She's wearing a plain black T-shirt, and her shorts are Sharpie-free. Her hair swings from a high ponytail and looks freshly washed. "Hey." She licks her lips, looking nervously toward the kitchen. "He's here. He's eating." She's shifting from foot to foot, practically wobbling back and forth with excitement. Or maybe she just really needs to pee. "He seems nice," she says in a low voice. "He said I'm the youngest fancier he's ever met."

"And this must be your partner." A man follows Sutton into the hall, still wiping crumbs from his chin with a napkin. I'm surprised to see that he's not much taller than me. "Grant Mueller," he says, holding out his hand. "Nice to meet you." Hovering behind him, Sutton's mom gives a little wave in my direction.

"Lauren Hall." I manage to introduce myself without squeaking too much. "Nice to meet you, too. But I'm not her partner. I mean, I'm just helping. She's the one who's done all the work."

"We're partners," Sutton says firmly. She shoots me a "shut up, already" kind of look.

"Well," Mr. Mueller says, "technically, we can only

have one name on the entry form. But Sutton here tells me you've been irreplaceable, training wise."

I can feel myself blushing.

"So." Mr. Mueller looks between us. "Should we start? We've got a tight schedule today. Thank you again for the muffins, Eva. Best I've ever had."

She smiles. "Secret family recipe."

"Eggnog," Sutton mouths at me as she follows the judge out the door. "Wait a minute," she says in her normal voice, pointing at the phone clutched in my hand. "Is that a cell? Did your parents finally realize the whole 'waiting until you're fourteen thing' is a terrible idea?"

"I wish," I say ruefully. "This is my mom's. I thought maybe I could film the Fly? You know, so your Dad can watch, too. And here." I thrust the papers I've been holding underneath my arm in Sutton's direction. "These are for you."

She takes the stack from me, looking confused.

"I made them for you. Well, Dad and me. They're drawings. I mean, not drawings. Plans. He's a structural engineer, so they should be, you know . . . okay."

Sutton looks down at the plans.

"It's the coop," I babble. "The 2.0 version. Look." I point at the large front section of the redesigned loft. "It's handicapped accessible. For when your dad gets home, for his wheelchair. He'll still be able to get inside, and everything. And Dad drew some plans for a ramp, too, for your house? He knows a guy, so he can get you a really, really good deal, and there are a couple different options for the walkway, but I think you'll want to go with . . ." I trail off. "Sorry. I should have asked. It's totally okay if you don't want any help. It was a bad— oof!"

The papers fly to the ground as Sutton slams into me, knocking the breath out of my lungs with a painful thwock. For a second, I think she's tackling me. But as her arms close around me, squeezing me like a cobra, I realize it's a hug.

Sutton's hugging me.

"Thank you," she whispers. "Thank you, thank you, thank you."

Pressing a slightly wet kiss to my cheek (I think she's actually crying a little, but it's hard to tell since I can't see her face), she gives me a final squeeze, then hurries off to catch up with the judge. I reach up to wipe my cheek.

Technically, that was my first kiss.

I make a mental note to tell Aiden later.

For some reason, as I make my toward the coop, I can't stop grinning.

CHAPTER 30

"READY WHENEVER YOU are," the judge calls out, holding his tally counter up in anticipation.

Sutton looks over at me, nervously straightening the end of her ponytail. "This is it, I guess."

"This is it," I echo. "You ready?" I hold Mom's cell up and start filming.

Sutton takes a deep breath. "Yeah. Count of three?"

"One," I obediently count. "Two. Three!"

She pulls open the gate.

For a minute, nothing happens.

Then, cautiously, the birds begin to spill out of the coop, winging their way upward. Sutton ducks inside, shooing the rest of the kit outside.

"Five minutes to time in," the judge tells us, watching as the kit begins to crisscross back and forth across the sky.

Sutton and I watch anxiously. The pigeons are starting to come together in a loose formation now, but they're not rolling yet.

What if they're still spooked from the hawk attack? What if they don't roll at all?

I tip my head back, searching for Crow.

The kit is soaring higher now. I lick my lips nervously. If they go too high, that's it. They'll just spend the entire twenty minutes doing laps above the coop.

Sutton reaches for my hand.

Come on, I chant in my head. *You can do it.*

I'm not sure which one of us is squeezing the other one's hand the hardest.

With less than a minute to go, the first bird drops.

"Crow," I say aloud. "It's Crow!"

"Time-in," Sutton shouts, dropping my hand. "Time-in!"

I tilt my head back, shielding my eyes.

As everyone watches, the rest of the birds launch themselves backward, following Crow's lead.

They're rolling.

ACKNOWLEDGMENTS

There aren't enough nice things to say about everyone who has helped turn *Roll* into an actual book. Enormous thanks to my amazing agent, Carrie Hannigan; I can't imagine where I would be without you. Thanks as well to Tanusri Prasanna, Danielle Burby, and everyone at HSG Agency.

A heartfelt thank you to Annie Berger for falling in love with *Roll*, as well as to my wonderful editor Jess MacLeish for being legitimately great at her job. Thanks to Becca Stadtlander and Kate Klimowicz for my awesome cover, and thanks to Veronica Ambrose and everyone at HarperCollins for the staggering amount of work that goes into publishing a novel.

Thanks to my dad, Wayne Feder, for not getting rid of his pigeons like he assured my mother he would before they were married. Thanks to my mom, Lynda Feder, for not getting rid of my dad in return.

Apologies to Wyle and Fitz for not putting any cats in the book.

And finally, thanks to my husband, Ben. You're pretty much the best in all possible ways.

REN'S PIGEON FACTS

↞ **PEOPLE HAVE BEEN RAISING PIGEONS** for longer than you'd probably think. Seriously. We're talking ancient Egypt here, people.

↞ **FAMOUS PIGEON FANCIERS INCLUDE** Walt Disney, Charles Darwin, and Queen Elizabeth II. The artist Pablo Picasso loved pigeons so much that he named his daughter "Paloma," the Spanish word for pigeon. So I guess I'm not the one whose dad gave them a terrible name.

↞ **WHILE BIRMINGHAM ROLLERS** tumble through the sky, another breed known as Parlor Rollers somersaults backward on the ground; they look like bowling balls. You should probably Google that right now.

→ **IN WORLD WAR II**, the allies used pigeons to carry messages behind enemy lines. Basically, pigeons used to be spies. A few of them even received medals for bravery.

→ **A FEW CENTURIES AGO**, pigeon poop was a big deal. People used it for fertilizer, and it was worth a *lot* of money. Armed guards used to stand outside of dovecotes (which is a fancy word for pigeon houses) and make sure no one stole it.

↞ **HEADS UP**: if you ever order "squab" at a restaurant, you'll be eating pigeon. So, you know . . . probably don't order squab.

↞ **SOME PIGEONS HAVE LIVED OVER FIFTEEN YEARS,** which is longer than most dogs. Plus, pigeons won't drool on you.

↞ **UNLESS THEY'RE SEPARATED FROM EACH OTHER,** pigeons tend to mate for life. Which means pigeon couples are probably together longer than most celebrity couples.

✦ **THE FASTEST PIGEON** on record flew over ninety miles per hour. That's faster than the speed limit! Well, in America, anyway.

✦ **SPEAKING OF FAST PIGEONS**, a champion racing pigeon named after Olympic athlete Usain Bolt once sold for over $400,000 dollars. Can you even imagine how many comic books you could buy with $400,000?

✦ **BIRMINGHAM ROLLERS WERE BRED** in the 1800s in Birmingham, England. Half of the members of Led Zeppelin also came from Birmingham. Sutton says that Led Zeppelin is a famous band from the seventies. She's pretty sure I wouldn't like their music.

← **OVER A THOUSAND OF THE WORLD'S TOP FANCIERS** from North America, Europe, Africa, and Australia compete in the annual World Cup Fly each year. A single judge spends over two months travelling from country to country in order to name the winner. Yep, two entire months. World Cup judges *really* like pigeons.

← **THE UNITED STATES' NATIONAL CHAMPIONSHIP FLY** is flown each fall to determine America's national champion. Sutton and I haven't won it . . . yet.